Robert Ayre

SKETCO
THE RAVEN

Scholastic Canada Ltd.
Toronto New York London Auckland Sydney
Mexico City New Delhi Hong Kong Buenos Aires

Scholastic Canada Ltd.
604 King Street West, Toronto, Ontario M5V 1E1, Canada

Scholastic Inc.
557 Broadway, New York, NY 10012, USA

Scholastic Australia Pty Limited
PO Box 579, Gosford, NSW 2250, Australia

Scholastic New Zealand Limited
Private Bag 94407, Botany, Manukau 2163, New Zealand

Scholastic Children's Books
Euston House, 24 Eversholt Street, London NW1 1DB, UK

Library and Archives Canada Cataloguing in Publication
Ayre, Robert, 1900-1980
    Sketco the raven / Robert Ayre.

Originally publ.: Toronto : Macmillan, 1961.
ISBN 978-1-4431-0044-1

    1. Indians of North America--Northwest Coast of
North America--Folklore--Juvenile literature. 2. Raven (Legendary
character)--Juvenile literature. I. Title.

PS8501.Y74S5 2009   398.2089'970711   C2009-905500-7

Text copyright © 1961 by Robert Ayre
Front cover image: © iStockphoto.com/Aarre Rinne

6 5 4 3 2 1   Printed in Canada   116   09 10 11 12 13

CONTENTS

To Thelma, "fellow-farer true through life,
heart-whole and soul-free," who has shared with me
the discovery of Canada. Our hikes in the Rockies
are remembered in these pages.

AUTHOR'S NOTE

The Raven Cycle of legends from which this narrative is drawn
was common to the Indians along the northern Pacific Coast, all
the way from the Asiatic side of Bering Strait to the southern part
of Vancouver Island. The smaller tribes, some of them living inland
from the sea, shared the tales with the great nations, the Tlingit of
Alaska, the Haida of the Queen Charlotte Islands, the Tsimshian of the
Skeena and the Nass, and the Kwakiutl, farther south. The Raven
was the hero, recognized by all, though he had many names and there
were variations in the telling of his adventures. The Tlingit called him
Yel, and he was Txamsem to the Tsimshian; on Vancouver Island, one
of his names was Meskwa, "The Greedy One"; but to the Bellabella
he was Hemaskas, "Real Chief"; the Haida called him Nankislas,
He "Whose Voice is Obeyed," and the Rivers Inlet people knew him
as Kwekwaxawe, "Great Inventor."

I have taken the name Sketco from the Tahltan Tsesketco,
"Great Raven" and, with the exception of Nass-shig-ee-yalth, which
is a simplification of the Tsimshian, the other names are also from
the Tahltan. These Athapaskan people, who controlled the upper
Stikine River drainage basin, traded with the Tlingit and in their
stories the Raven spoke the Tlingit tongue.

While I have used my imagination in re-creating the Raven tales,
I have endeavoured to be true to the life and character of the people
who told them and, confident in the authenticity of my version, I pay
my respects to the ethnologists who collected them from the Indians,
with particular gratitude to Franz Boas, James A. Teit, Diamond
Jenness and Marius Barbeau.

Robert Ayre, 1961

CHAPTER 1

HOW THE RAVEN STOLE THE STARS

Once upon a time, long before the White Man was born, no one lived in Canada but the Indians and the wild animals, and they lived in utter darkness. The Great Chief, Nass-shig-ee-yalth, and his friends dwelt by themselves at the mouth of a river in the North and hoarded all the light. The stars Nass-shig-ee-yalth kept hidden in a bag and he treasured the sun and the moon in two boxes, one painted with silver paint and the other gilded with gold. The Great Chief was proud of his possessions and he loved to pore over them as misers pore over their riches. "I am a wealthy man!" he would boast, as he undid the string of his bag and ran his fingers through the glittering stars. "I am the richest man in the world! Look, my friends!" He was fond of astonishing his friends and they never ceased being amazed, no matter how often he revealed the light to them. He would beckon them to his side, and while they gathered close and watched him loosening the lid of one of the boxes, he would look up at them with a sly smile. Suddenly he would move his hand and the light of the sun or of the moon would pour out of the box in such a blaze of glory that it would seem as if the house were afire and the men would stagger back blinded. Nass-shig-ee-yalth would laugh and clap the lid on the box, and never would he tire of playing this game.

But the poor Indians in the world outside sat huddled in the darkness and cold, shivering and hungry, because they had no fires and they could not see to hunt. All they could do was grope about in the blackness and find roots and berries with their fingers, dry, tough roots and green berries that could never ripen. They were in a miserable plight, but they thought their wretchedness was ordained by the Spirits, for they knew nothing of sun, moon or stars. Had they known that there was such a thing as light, they would have imagined that they were all born blind in a blind world.

The Great Chief was aware of their misery but it made him all the more vain and arrogant. "See how poor and cold and hungry and naked they are!" said he. "And see how powerful am I!"

"Will you not lend them some of your light?" asked

one of his friends, who had a soft heart.

Nass-shig-ee-yalth turned upon him in a fury. "Not a star!" he cried.

But there was one being who took pity on the plight of the poor Indians, and this was the Raven, who flew about the world and had eyes so sharp that he could pierce the darkest gloom. Beyond the rim of the world, in the high North, in the North beyond the North, Sketco, the Raven, was born. He flew out of his own land and was soaring over the river near the borders one day when he saw a gleam of light dart up into the black sky. The Great Chief was showing his sun to his friends and the light flashed through the smoke-hole in the roof. The light flashed and disappeared, and the Raven heard the Great Chief laugh.

Sketco wheeled and dropped closer to the roof. Then he poised on his broad wings and peered in through the smoke-hole. He saw Nass-shig-ee-yalth gleefully undoing the string of his bag. Nass-shig-ee-yalth's grin was lit up by a radiant glow as he opened the mouth of the bag. He turned the bag upside down and poured the stars out on the ground. Some of them lay in a dazzling heap and others rolled helter-skelter everywhere, dancing and twinkling and sparkling and making such a light that the Raven could see every wrinkle of Nass-shig-ee-yalth's leering face and could count his yellow teeth. The Great Chief gathered up the stars in his brown hands and fingered them lovingly before he put them back in the bag. When one of the children darted forward to help him pick them up, he shouted so angrily that the poor child fled in terror.

A great rage took hold of the Raven's heart as he saw the miser hoarding all the light of the world and he thought of the hapless Indians crouching in the darkness. He flew away but he resolved to come back and steal the stars.

When the Great Chief was sleeping by his smouldering fire that night, the Raven stole in through the smoke-hole. He saw a bag hanging from the rafters, which he thought was the bag of stars, and, quickly seizing it with his beak, he jerked it away and flew off with it. But he soon knew, from the smell that came out of the bag, that he had made a mistake. He had stolen a bundle of dried fish. As soon as he perceived this, he opened his beak and let his burden drop. It fell into the midst of a starving family that sat shuddering and blind beside the fearful tumultuous ocean and knew nothing of fish. But the poor Indians seized the bag and tore it open and devoured every shred. The story of the miraculous fall from heaven passed rapidly from Indian to Indian and tribe to tribe, until all the Indians in

Canada were gazing up sightless into the unbroken black sky and holding out their hands in the hope that heaven would open again and more food might drop down.

Once again, Sketco let himself into the house of Nass-shig-ee-yalth to steal the light for poor mortals, but this time the Great Chief awakened and caught sight of him as he flew in. With a cry of surprise, the Great Chief sprang up and clutched at the Raven. But the bird was too swift for him. He sprang into the air, dodged, and with one stroke of his great black wings vanished through the hole in the roof. Nass-shig-ee-yalth was left with a glossy tail-feather in his fingers. He did not know, of course, what had brought the Raven into the house, but like all misers he was afraid that his treasure was in danger. So he sent orders throughout his village that any large black bird that was seen must be killed instantly, and he kept the sun, the moon and the stars closer than ever. He enjoyed them now in secret, and forbade anyone to enter on pain of death. In secret he gloated more than ever over his blazing sun, his silver-glowing moon and his sparkling stars, and he cherished them all the more because he feared that he might lose them.

But the Raven, going about the earth and seeing the famished Indians shuddering in the dark and stretching up their bony hands to the unyielding sky, was more determined than ever to bring them the warm sun for their well-being and the moon and stars for their delight. He said nothing to them but he schemed both night and day.

At last he hit upon a plan and he lost no time in returning to the village of Nass-shig-ee-yalth. A band of boys playing in the woods saw the Raven appear and remembering the Great Chief's command they shouted and fell upon the bird with sticks and stones. Sorely hurt, Sketco managed to struggle into the topmost branches of a lofty pine tree. Two of the boys began swarming up the tree, while the others kept watch, ready to fling stones if he should take to the wing. But before they could reach him, the Raven had vanished. He had turned himself into a pine needle.

The boys were dumbfounded and they were more frightened when they realized that in their chase through the forest they had come to the forbidden spring, where none might drink but the daughter of the Great Chief. With swift glances at the pine tree and at the spring which bubbled up from its roots, the boys ran away. They agreed among themselves to say nothing about the black bird, for fear of being punished.

Now the cunning Raven, for all he was a pine needle

clinging to a limb of the tall tree in the forest, could still see, and he kept watch for the daughter of Nass-shig-ee-yalth. Late in the day she came, with her companions. They had been picking berries all afternoon and they were weary and thirsty. They all threw themselves down on the ground whilst the daughter of the Great Chief knelt to drink at the spring. At that moment, Sketco freed himself from his twig and let himself fall into the water. In her hurry to quench her thirst, the princess scooped up the pine needle in her hand and swallowed it with the cool water. But she did not know that she had swallowed a pine needle and she knew nothing of the Good Spirit who had schemed to save mankind.

The daughter of Nass-shig-ee-yalth went home to her father's house and in the course of time she fell ill and gave birth to a child. It was a little dusky Indian boy and it was received with rejoicing in the village of the Great Chief. But no one knew that it was the Raven, who had turned himself into a pine needle and had now become the grandson of Nass-shig-ee-yalth in order to steal the sun for the poor mortals who crouched in darkness.

The proud grandfather gave a feast to all his friends. In a burst of vanity and generosity, he hung up both the sun and the moon on poles outside his house and the people danced all night, with faces shining as never before, and their long black shadows danced violently with them to the steady thump of the drums. It was then that the Indians crawling about the earth saw light for the first time. In the remote distance it flickered against the heavy pall of the sky, as frail and elusive as the northern lights when they shine but dimly. At first the Indians were aghast and they fell on their faces in terror, but after a time they took courage and sat peering at the ghostly movement on the sky, murmuring among themselves and hoping for new wonders.

"The meaning of it," said one of the shamans, one of the medicine men, "is that the heaven is moving. It is loosening. The sky will gape open and more food will fall down upon us."

"We shall eat! We shall eat!" cried the Indians, and they began to dance for joy. But they soon fell down exhausted.

Nass-shig-ee-yalth took down the sun and laid it carefully in the gilded box, and he took down the moon and stowed it away in the silver box. He put the lids on and fastened them, and all this before he thought of sleep. Thus the light vanished, and the poor Indians, when they saw it die out of the sky, sank down in bitter despair.

But Sketco had not forgotten them. He grew quickly and was soon a sturdy lad running about his grandfather's house, playing games in the woods with the other children. Nass-shig-ee-yalth was proud of him and loved him next to the sun and the moon.

"What is it that you keep in that beautiful glittering bag, Grandfather?" asked the Raven one day, when the old Chief sat stroking his hair.

Nass-shig-ee-yalth took the little boy's face in his hands and looked into his dark eyes. But he could read nothing there of the cunning of the Raven.

"What makes you ask, my boy?"

"Because the bag shines so, Grandfather. I can see it hanging in the dark."

Said the Great Chief: "It is a mighty secret, son." He drew the boy close to him and whispered in his ear: "I have the stars in that bag!"

But the clever Raven pretended that he did not understand, so Nass-shig-ee-yalth lifted down the bag and unfastened the string that bound it.

"Hold out your two hands," he invited. The boy cupped his small brown palms together and held them out and the grandfather filled them with stars. They were heavy and warm and how they glittered and sparkled!

The Great Chief laughed to see the look of astonishment and delight on the boy's face, and he poured out the stars until they brimmed over and fell to the ground.

Thereafter, the Raven was allowed to play with the stars, and he was always careful of them, as he kneeled on the ground and fashioned them into scintillating designs, such as circles and triangles and the shapes of men and deer. He set them out in rows, too, and rolled them about, playing games with them, as if they were common marbles instead of the brilliant stars of heaven. Whenever he was weary of his play, he gathered them up and counted them one by one into the bag, and Nass-shig-ee-yalth watched with his sharp eyes to see that none was lost.

All this time, Sketco was plotting to steal the stars, for while he had the body of a little Indian boy, he was still the Raven and he still bore in his heart the picture of the poor earthly mortals engulfed in the fathomless dark.

So one night, when the Great Chief was asleep, and the Great Chief's daughter was fast in slumber, the little grandson wriggled out of his blankets and stole softly to where the bag of stars was hanging. Without a sound, he unfastened the bag and took it down. He let it sink to the ground, for it was heavy, and crouched, with ears strained to catch the faintest sound. He tiptoed to the door and crawled out. All was dark and still in the village. Moving as stealthily as a shadow, he laid hold of the bag of stars and dragged it out. No sooner was he in the open than he stretched out his arms and rose on his toes and changed himself back into his own shape. In his beak he clutched the precious burden firmly, and with one sweep of his mighty black wings, the Raven soared into the night sky.

Higher, higher and higher soared the Raven, until he was miles and leagues above the dark earth. Suddenly he opened his bill. The bag fell and dropped like a plummet. In its swiftness it burst and showered the sky with stars. They fell in a silver hailstorm and as they fell each star burst and was scattered in a thousand smaller stars, until the whole heaven was overspread with them. The sky that had been black was now glittering from end to end with millions of stars shooting and bursting like rockets.

The Indians, frightened out of their wits, ran hither and thither, and threw themselves on their faces. Some of them dashed into the sea and were drowned; some frantically began clawing up the earth with their fingers so as to bury themselves. When some of them had regained their courage, they cast terrified glances at the sky, and then, hidden in the trees, stared outright at it.

But the stars did not fall on them, for so high was the

Raven when he dropped the bag that, when they stopped falling, the stars remained hanging in the sky.

"Have no fear," said the shamans. "The Spirits have riddled the sky with holes and soon it will be torn asunder. Then will the food fall through to us."

For days and nights the Indians gazed up at the starry sky in wonder and awe. No food fell down out of heaven, but they got comfort out of staring at the stars and inventing stories about the strange patterns they made in silver across the great spread of darkness.

In the meantime, Sketco flew down to the village of Nass-shig-ee-yalth and when he lighted in front of the Great Chief's house he changed as quickly as his feet touched the ground into the form of the little grandson again. Without the slightest sound, he crept in and crawled into his blankets.

He pretended to be asleep. Of a sudden, he screamed. His mother, startled, jumped up and ran to him, with his grandfather at her heels.

"What ails you, little son?" asked the Chief's daughter, clasping the child to her breast and stroking his hair soothingly. The boy cried and could not answer.

"He has been dreaming," grunted Nass-shig-ee-yalth.

When he had been quieted at last, the little boy, the

cunning Raven, sobbed out his story.

"I was lying asleep," he said, "when I was awakened by a noise like the rushing wind."

"Dreams," soothed the mother. "It is a still night, and your grandfather and I were asleep until we heard you call."

"It was like the roar of wind and thunder," said the child. "I was terribly afraid. Suddenly the house opened at the top and the whole thing fell down."

"The house stands whole," said Nass-shig-ee-yalth. "See for yourself, little grandson. You have been having a nightmare."

"A great black bird with widespread wings that seemed to fill the sky came in."

The Great Chief frowned and listened intently.

"He snatched the bag of stars with his beak and flew away. I could not stop him. I was so frightened I could not move. Then I screamed."

The boy began crying afresh and his mother could not comfort him.

"The stars are gone, the stars are gone!" he cried.

"No, no," said the Great Chief's daughter. "It was all a dream. See, your grandfather will bring the stars to you again."

Nass-shig-ee-yalth strode across the floor to the rafter

where the stars had hung. He started back in astonishment. The bag was gone. He shouted and began a frantic search. The mother watched him, amazed, and the child went on weeping.

In consternation, the Great Chief roused the whole village and had torches lit and every man, woman and child scatter abroad in the search. "Tear up every bush!" he commanded. "Cut down every tree! Leave no stone unturned! Burn the grass! Drain the rivers dry!"

The hunt went on in great excitement, while Sketco cried bitterly, as if he had lost the thing nearest his heart instead of gaining it, and the Great Chief stormed up and down.

At last, a boy, happening to look up instead of down, spied the stars ranged in splendour far aloft above the tallest totem poles, and called out for all to look. The searchers stopped and stared up into the sky and Nass-shig-ee-yalth came out and stood with folded arms and stared up into the sky with a heavy frown on his face which soon turned into a contortion of rage. Hearing the tumult, the little grandson ran out of the house and stretched up his hands and jumped, and when he found he could not reach the stars, cried louder than ever. But all the time he was laughing in his Raven heart.

The Great Chief ordered the tallest trees to be climbed – for they had not all been cut down – but even the longest arm, thrusting out the longest pole, from the top of the tallest tree, could not touch the nearest star. Nass-shig-ee-yalth marched into his house and there he drew his blanket round him and sat glowering and sulking for hours. He sent out orders that the closest watch was to be kept about the village and commanded that if the great black bird appeared again and was allowed to escape, every man on guard was to be tied to a tree and made to bristle with spears as a porcupine with quills.

CHAPTER 2

HOW HE STOLE THE MOON AND THE SUN

In time, the Raven ceased his weeping, but he refused to eat and fell thin and looked so peaked and sorrowful that his mother's heart was wrung to see him, and she entreated the Great Chief to give him something else to play with.

But Nass-shig-ee-yalth was afraid of losing his other treasures, so his heart was stone.

"Have pity!" cried the mother. "It was not the child's fault that the stars were stolen! Would you see him die of longing? Lift the lid of the silver box and let him look at the moon!"

"No," said the Chief.

"One look will not harm the moon," pleaded the mother.

"No."

"Are you afraid of a bird? Get your shamans, get your

bravest fighters, your most powerful magic, your strongest arms and your sharpest spears, and hedge the moon about with them. Then lift the lid yourself. I will answer for the moon with my life. Can't you see that the child is dying?"

In the end, the stubborn Chief relented. He summoned his hunters and his medicine men, and they came with their bows and arrows and their war clubs and their rattles and their charms; they came in their paint and they came in their beads, and they all wore terrible frowns, for they were afraid and they knew not what to do. While they stood in a solid bodyguard, the hunters with tight lips and the priests with mouths muttering, the Great Chief dragged out the silver box and lifted the lid. The light of the moon burst out of the box and rose like a cloud, flooding the house with glory, and the little grandson laughed and clapped his hands and danced up and down with joy. The moon lay at the bottom of the chest like an immense round shield, cool but burnished and shining with a great shine.

"You see how it cheers him," said the mother, glancing fondly at the boy. "He will not die now."

They could not tear the grandson away from the moon. He crouched before it, gazing at it and stroking it and patting it with his hands. The shamans and the hunters grew weary standing. The hunters pressed their lips tighter together and shifted from one foot to the other, and the shamans muttered louder and invented a curse against all birds, so that they could chant it and relieve their feelings. All the while, the Raven was scheming in his heart a plan to steal the moon, for he did not think that the stars were enough light for mankind. But he knew that his task would be much harder now.

At last, he fell asleep and was carried off to bed. The shamans and the hunters were released and a second shift was brought in to take their places guarding the moon; and the sun as well.

As the days passed by and there was no sign of the Raven, vigilance relaxed a little and the grandson was allowed to take the moon out of the box and trundle it about like a wheel. But wherever he went, there were strong, swift men with him to keep watch.

To fly with the moon was impossible. If he turned into his own form he would have to do so before the eyes of the bodyguard, and even if he escaped the spears and swift arrows, he would never be able to come back for the sun. And Sketco had made up his mind that he would bring the sun, moon and stars to the Indians. So Sketco ran up and down with the shining moon every day, rolling it before him and having the braves roll it back to him, and spinning it, and every moment as he played, trying to think of a way to deceive the swift, strong men with the keen eyes. At last he thought of a plan.

He tried to toss the moon into the air one day when he was out in the woods, but could not, for he was too small, so he laughed and said: "Which of you can throw the farthest?"

The hunters looked at one another and said they would not throw. The Raven then taunted them, until one of the men stepped proudly forward and, without a word, took the moon in his hand and swung his arm in a wide circle. The moon left his fingers and soared into the air, spinning and flashing with silver radiance. High above the tree-tops it flew. It seemed to hang a moment before it curved and plunged down to earth again.

Sketco laughed and clapped his hands and said: "No one can beat that! None of you can throw higher than that! Toss it again!"

Another hunter strode out and picked up the moon. He was a great braggart and he swaggered as he lifted the disc, and he nodded his head and leered, as if to say, "Watch me!" He held the moon in his curved fingers and crouched low like a discus thrower. He held his breath and strained all the muscles of his body so tensely that the sweat stood shining on his forehead. The other braves smiled to themselves. With a mighty effort, the braggart lunged into the air and heaved the moon above his head. He fell back on the ground but the moon sailed up, up and up, dizzily spinning and casting off a rapidly flickering light.

Rising to his feet, the braggart grinned in vanity at the astonishment of the other strong men, for the moon was far beyond the tips of the loftiest trees and was still flying. The higher it rose, the brighter was the light it shed. The thrower's triumph was turned to consternation, and when he saw that the moon would not come down again, he threw himself on the ground in terror. He would have fled, but the hunters marched up to him grimly and fastened their fingers on his arms and shoulders. The Raven, pretending once more to be stricken with grief, was weeping as though his heart would break.

But the poor mortal Indians saw the moon rise out of the earth and swing higher and higher into the starry heaven and they shouted with delight. They watched it soar and looked for it to burst into a thousand stars, but it dimmed the sparkle of the stars by its own enchantment and filled all the earth with a soft silvery glow as it slowly climbed the sky, circled across it and sank steadily down to the earth again on the other side.

The Indians then wept and lamented, but next night the moon appeared again, and night after night thereafter, for so strong was the arm of the braggart – or so great the magic of the Raven – that the moon never stopped but kept on going round and round the earth forever.

But the braggart, because he had lost the moon, was dragged before Nass-shig-ee-yalth, cowering in fear, and he was judged and afterwards struck down by a whalebone club and killed.

In the light of the moon, the Indians discovered the wild animals who had themselves come out of their dens to see the wonders, and learned how to sharpen stones and make weapons to hunt down the beasts and kill them. Thus they got meat, but they had no fire, so they ate it raw.

It was the crafty Sketco's ambition to bring them the sun, as he had brought them the stars and the moon, and he set about his purpose by crying and falling ill because he no longer had his moon for a plaything. In the end, the Great Chief could not refuse him, but he would not let the boy take the sun out of the box.

"I have lost my stars and I have lost my moon," he

said. "Must I lose the greatest treasure of all, my sun? How is it that we, the Great People, have been able to live in comfort, while the Indians in the darkness starved and perished of cold? The insignificant mortals grovel in holes in the ground and chew bark and roots, while we dwell in houses and fish in the sea and eat good food. Why is this? Because we have had the light. Even when I kept the sun and the moon sealed up in my chests, we had light throughout our village and in all our woods, and out across the sea, so powerful was the magic of my treasures. Now the stars are out of reach and the moon has gone rolling up the sky! The miserable Indians are now greedily devouring my light and soon I shall have none left. If they get my sun, we shall be no better off than they are. Instead of owning it, we shall have to share it. They will be as happy and as strong as we are. They may even sweep down upon us and destroy us!"

So the Great Chief would lift the lid of the sun box and allow the grandson to peep in at the magnificent ball of fire, but no more. And he called upon the shamans to weave strange dances round and round the box. With crowns of grizzly bear claws on their heads, and hideous masks on their faces and paint on their wrists and arms and legs, with strings of beads round their necks, and with

rattles in their bony fingers, they shuffled back and forward, round and round, writhing and chanting, and doing their best to keep the sun safe for the Great Chief. But
their medicine was of no avail against the medicine of the
Raven.

He was not afraid now to reveal himself, for if he could
escape with the sun he would have all he wanted. To get
the sun he would have to make a bold stroke. After thinking about it long and intently, he ran out into the woods,
transformed himself into his own shape and spread his
wings for all the village to see. The village sprang alive
with scurry and shout; the hunters grasped their bows and
the urchins picked up sticks and stones; the Great Chief
hurried out and the shamans emerged and ranged themselves in line, calling down blood-curdling curses on the
great black bird soaring overhead. Sketco flew off toward
the North and the people poured pell-mell after him. Suddenly the Raven dropped down and, while the hunters
were beating the woods frantically to corner him, changed
into the shape of the grandson again. So intent was everyone on the hunt that no one noticed the little boy dodging
through the woods and darting back to the village.

He burst into the deserted house of Nass-shig-ee-yalth
and, without stopping for breath, tugged at the golden

chest and pried off the lid. The sun lay in the box like a ball of soft gold. The Raven did not stop to admire it. With much effort, for he was only a small boy with short puny arms, he managed to overturn the box and dump the sun out on the earth. The great globe, blazing with such a light that it almost blinded him, rolled out of the door, and he ran after it, trembling with fear that he might lose it or that the villagers might see the light. What to do with the sun now that he had it, Sketco did not know. As a little Indian boy, he could not carry it in his arms or upon his back: if he transformed himself into his own shape, he could not fly with the enormous burden of the round, burning sun. Because it was so heavy, it rolled only a few yards away, and there it lay on the earth pouring out the glory of its light and deluging the village and all the woods around. The Great Chief and the hunters, the shamans, the women and the little children stopped in their tracks and then, at a hoarse word, began running headlong back to the village.

The Raven heard the shouts, and his heart stopped in his breast, but he quickly overcame his fright and found his voice.

He stood over the sun and cried: *"Fly, Sun, fly!"*

He glanced up and saw that three hunters, panting and sweating and grasping their war clubs until their knuckles were white, were tearing through the woods.

"Sun, Sun, Sun!" the Raven sang, clenching his hands and pressing his heels into the ground. *"No clod of earth are you! Break loose, leap up and fly!"*

One of the hunters stumbled and one turned quickly to lift him, but the third ran on. Closer and closer he pressed to where the Great Chief's little grandson, to where Sket-co the Raven stood singing frantically to the burning sun. Behind the three hunters, coming more slowly but coming relentlessly, crowded Nass-shig-ee-yalth and the whole village.

The Raven, with his body as taut as a bowstring straining against an arrow, swayed backwards and forwards over the sun and stretched his tense fingers down to it and then suddenly relaxed and threw back his head and gazed into the sky.

"Sun! Sun! Sun!" he shouted. *"No frozen stone are you! Break loose, leap up and fly!"*

The sun seemed to shift and begin to revolve slowly as his voice rose. The hunters pushed forward ruthlessly, for they could see that the little grandson was trying to weave magic about the sun. But they dared not throw their clubs at him, for he was the grandson of Nass-shig-ee-yalth and they were afraid to shed his blood.

Rapidly and more rapidly, so that his words seemed to be lost in a spinning of sound, the Raven sang, imploring the sun to launch itself into the sky, calling upon the ball of fire to leap up and swerve high over the village, to soar up and out of reach, as the moon had soared. The sun moved. Slowly it began to rise from the ground. The Raven sang with never a pause for breath. Time seemed to stop, and the hunters, while they forced their way relentlessly forward, seemed to come not a step nearer. The Raven sang of the piteous Indians huddling cold in the dark and called upon the sun to shower its mercy upon them. He sang of the glorious expanse of heaven where the sun could rove, no longer kept shut up in a box to be brought out at the behest and the whim of a vain and avaricious man. He sang and beat his hands in rhythm. He sang and swayed his body in rhythm. Slowly, steadily, the sun floated up. It rose above the totem poles. It rose above the treetops.

As if suddenly jerked out of a spell, the hunters shouted and the shamans screamed. Nass-shig-ee-yalth groaned and cried out: "Kill the boy! He is no son of mine! He is a devil, he is a devil! Kill him and bring me back my sun!" But the Raven went on singing and swaying, exulting in his heart. The Great Chief rushed forward to strike him down, but the Great Chief's daughter clutched his arm and held him back. A spear flew over the Raven's head and sank shivering into a tree trunk. Panting and sweating, two hunters fell upon the Raven and the villagers pressed in around them. Sketco laughed and shouted. The floating sun leapt in the air as if it were a stone flung from a sling. The Raven shouted again and the sun shot up like a rocket, like a comet, leaving a train of sparks behind it.

The hunters fastened their hands on the little Indian boy and, Nass-shig-ee-yalth, shaking free from the mother, strode forward, his face black with anger. But just as they touched him, he was a little Indian boy no longer. In their hands, as quick as a dart of lightning, he changed into the Raven. His black wings beat in their face. He shook his feathers and plunged into the air. The hunters fell back, affrighted. All the villagers cried out in surprise and alarm, and by the time their wits came back to them and they understood the Great Chief's shouts and began shooting with their arrows and hurtling stones and fish spears and clubs into the air, the Raven was far out of reach.

Before the eyes of Nass-shig-ee-yalth and his hunters and shamans, the sun climbed higher and higher, dwindling, shrinking, until it was no more than a bright jewel glittering in the sky. The Raven appeared in the light for a moment, like a black speck, so high had he soared, and then in a twinkling, he vanished.

So it was the Raven charmed the sun away from the miser Nass-shig-ee-yalth for the welfare of the whole world. The Indians squatting and trembling by the sea were amazed when the sun rose upon them for the first time. Brighter far than the moon, brighter than the stars, it wiped out both moon and stars. In its glory it swallowed them. The sky was suffused with blue. The sea shone and sparkled. The green grass pushed up through the black earth. The withered trees felt the sap running through their veins and trembled and burst like song into green leaf. The flowers showered the earth with colour and sweetened the air with perfume. For the first time, the Indians saw each other's faces in the full light. They laughed and danced and sang. They were no longer cold. No longer were they blind. The poor mortals were wretched no more. They began at last to live. When the sun disappeared at night, they lamented, but they had the moon and the stars for their consolation and they were weary with finding life, so they slept; and when they awakened again the sun swung round the earth and lighted them to fresh joy. Day in and day out, the sun circled the heaven and served them with warmth and light, and the earth burgeoned for them, and the Raven, who stole for them the moon, the sun and the stars, lived throughout history and for all time in their tales.

CHAPTER 3

SKETCO BEGINS HIS WANDERINGS

Beyond the rim of the world, in the high North, in the North beyond the North, Sketco the Raven was born. Sketco was the youngest of four brothers, but the others were all murdered by their uncle, one after the other, and he would have murdered Sketco, too, had the Raven not been so cunning.

"I am going out fishing," the uncle would say to his sister. "Let me take one of the boys with me to steer the canoe."

"Very well," said the mother, and the uncle plodded down the narrow trail and over the sand to the ocean, with his paddles upon his shoulder and one of the sturdy boys at his heels carrying the net.

The boy hopped lightly into the canoe and the uncle shoved it out into the water and jumped in himself. With one stroke of the paddle, he sent it spinning out across the sea and the little nephew laughed to see how swiftly it flew over the water and how small the houses of the village looked among the trees.

"Shall I spread the net, Uncle?" he asked, but the uncle only grunted and plucked the water again with a firm sweep of the paddle.

They were now far out at sea and the boy grew a little frightened as he saw the deep swirling waters gathering round them from as far as eye could reach. He had never been such a long way from land before and he laughed nervously and said, to keep up his courage: "Why don't you laugh, Uncle? See how the waves shoulder each other! Are they wrestling?" His teeth chattered and he clutched the sides of the canoe with both hands, but he said: "Isn't it fun, Uncle?"

The uncle scowled and a lock of his lank black hair lay across his cheek like an ugly scar. Once more he dipped the paddle and sent the canoe tossing in the waves that were swelling more and more boisterously.

The little boy shrank and his eyes were wide open with fear. "They are getting rough, Uncle!" he cried, and he ducked his head as one of the waves threw its wet weight against the canoe and rudely forced it back. The cold water splashed the boy's bare knees and the shock made him shiver.

"Take me home, Uncle!" he pleaded.

The uncle grinned but the boy was more terrified of the grin than he was of the man's scowl, and he buried his head in his arms and sobbed. The canoe heaved and pitched and the waves battered it with resounding thunderclaps. Terrified and cold, and deathly sick, the little nephew lay curled up in the bottom. Suddenly, the uncle lurched violently and turned the canoe over. The boy screamed as he was plunged into the sea, but the wicked uncle only leered the more as he tossed his hair back and struck out swimming to catch the canoe, which was bobbing upside down on the heavy waves. He grasped it and set it right; then he climbed in and paddled for home.

"Where is my son?" cried the mother, when she saw him striding up the trail alone with his net over one arm and his paddles on his shoulder. She saw that he was dripping wet and she shrieked and clutched at him and demanded where the boy was.

The uncle shrugged his shoulders and stalked on. "Where are my fish?" he asked grimly.

The mother, following him and pulling at his net to make him stop, screamed and threw herself on the ground.

"I took him out to help me fish," her brother said,

turning and looking down at her coldly. "Where are the fish? The net is empty. Your boy was worse than useless. You have others, better than he was, I hope. Worse than useless," he muttered. "He jumped about and upset the canoe. I might have been drowned. And now I have had the trip for nothing." He turned on his heel and went away grumbling, leaving the poor mother to tear at the grass and beat the ground in her grief.

The boy's father came home from hunting to find that his little son had been drowned, but he did not blame the uncle because he was himself a good-natured man and he did not suspect that the uncle had a spite against him.

The mother did not blame him, either, because he was her brother, so when he came to her again and said: "I am going out fishing; let me take one of the other boys to steer the canoe," she consented. First of all, she winced and said "No."

"What!" said the uncle. "Are you afraid to trust him with me? The other boy was a little fool, but this fellow is strong and he has a steady head on his shoulders. It is time he learned to fish, a lad of his age."

"Let him go," said the boy's father. "I am ashamed, Brother-in-law, that a son of mine should have failed you. This boy will do better."

"Let me go, Mother," said the child. "I will be careful, and I will bring you home a big salmon."

So the mother yielded, and the second son jumped into the canoe and was soon speeding across the sea.

"Tell me when to spread the net, Uncle," said the boy. "I am eager to become a great fisherman like you."

The uncle grunted and the boy peered over the side of the canoe, trying to see the fish in the deep black water.

"I saw something flicker!" he cried with excitement. "Shall I let the net out?"

"Look again," said the uncle laconically.

"I see it! I see it!"

"Take care you don't lean over too far and tip the canoe," said the uncle. As he spoke he jumped up suddenly and pushed the little nephew over the edge. Without a cry, the boy sank into the depths of the sea.

The mother was anxiously waiting, and when she saw the uncle climbing up the trail with his net on his arm and his paddles over his shoulder, she cried aloud and would not be comforted. All night long, the whole village wailed and moaned for the lost boy, all except the uncle, who sulked in his blanket and declared that he would never take another boy out to help him fish.

When the father returned from his hunting trip, he

went to the uncle and said: "Brother-in-law, I am disgraced at having two sons so weak and helpless as these have been." The uncle grunted and looked down at the net he was mending. "I have one son left. Take him . . ."

"No," said the uncle, without looking up.

"He is a good boy. Take him so that the honour of the family may be redeemed. I will speak to him so that he will be on his best behaviour."

The father persuaded the uncle to take the third lad out to sea with him but when he spoke of it, the boy gaped at him and then ran and hid himself. His mother cried: "No! no! I will not let him leave my sight! I will not let him go! He is the only child I have left."

"Do you want to make a woman out of him?" the father demanded angrily.

"If you must make him into a man," sobbed the mother, "take him into the woods with you, but I will not let him go on the water. He will be drowned as the others were drowned."

But the father had his way and the child was dragged out and carried to the canoe.

There he sat shivering, without a sound, while the uncle paddled, watching him out of the corner of his eye, until they were far from sight of land.

"You are not a bright companion," said the uncle, with ugly pleasantry.

The boy winced but did not answer and did not look at him.

"You won't answer? Well, keep quiet, then!" The man turned wrathfully and knocked his nephew into the sea with the paddle.

The poor mother was not surprised to hear that her third son had been drowned, but she grieved more than ever and the village mourned with her.

Time went by and the mother gave birth to another son, and this was Sketco, the Raven.

From his childhood, he was not like the other boys of the village. Perhaps it was because he was so carefully cherished by his mother and father. He would go into the woods hunting with his father, but he would not play, except by himself, and the game he liked best was a strange one: he loved to carve tiny canoes out of wood, and fish, and men and animals as well, and, although he kept it all secret to himself, he could make his wooden fish swim in the puddles and he had the power to cause his men and animals to walk. He fed them on small chips of wood and bark and they moved only when they felt the touch of his warm fingers.

Sketco grew and the uncle looked on him with envious eyes. At last, one day, when the boy's father was away hunting, the uncle came and said to Sketco: "Would you like to come fishing with me?"

Sketco looked at his tight-closed mouth and at the piercing black eyes under his cruel brows, and Sketco knew what was in his heart.

"Yes," he said, with a quick smile, and he ran to tell his mother.

"He shall not go with you," said the mother firmly. "The sea has swallowed up three of my sons and Sketco is the only one I have left. His father is a patient man, but he would be angry if he came home from the hunt and found that he, too, had been drowned. No. Steer the canoe yourself, or else get some other boy."

"I have taken other boys," said the uncle sourly. "Nothing has harmed them. Your three lads were at fault. One was foolish and one was reckless and the other dropped into the sea out of sheer fright. "Bah!" he said and he spat on the ground in disgust. "What can I expect from such a father as theirs?"

"That is no way to speak of my father!" cried Sketco, clenching his fist. "When he comes home, he will kill you!"

"Hush!" chided his mother.

"I am not afraid to go with my uncle!" the boy exclaimed.

"You speak as if you were made of manly stuff," said the uncle, with a leer which was meant to be a smile. "I will make a good fisherman of you, and you will be a pride to your father."

"No harm will come to me, Mother," said Sketco.

He spoke with such confidence that he prevailed upon her and she let him go, although her heart was heavy.

But before Sketco followed his uncle down the path to the shore, he took one of the little toy canoes he had carved and hid it in the folds of his blanket.

"I am ready, Uncle!" he shouted. "Get in and I will push off."

The uncle looked at him, surprised at his boldness, but he climbed in. He was about to jeer at the boy, but Sketco shoved the canoe into the water as if he had the strength of a man. He leapt in and said: "Give me the paddle, Uncle!" The man studied him with piercing black eyes and answered: "No."

He looked at the boy with suspicion as he dipped the paddle in the sea and sent the canoe shooting out over the water.

"How far shall we go?" asked Sketco. The wind blew his dark hair back and his eyes shone with delight.

"Far," said the uncle without looking up.

The canoe raced across the sea so rapidly that the shore fled behind and disappeared. One moment they saw a rocky island, dishevelled with haggling, screeching gulls, rise up before them; the next moment it was a dark spot on the ocean and they could not hear the screaming nor see the white wings; and in a twinkling, the island had been swallowed up as if it had never existed.

"We are racing the wind!" cried Sketco.

The uncle grunted.

The long leagues of the ocean rolled east and west and north and south, and all the life Sketco could see in the wilderness of waters was a solitary whale spouting in the sun far away on the horizon.

"Shall we catch the whale?" he asked.

For answer, the uncle suddenly jumped up and struck the boy with the paddle, toppling him over into the se He laughed and switched the canoe around, to sc homeward.

Down, down, down sank Sketco. The water cl over him and around him as if it would crush him. Sketco was not taken unawares as his hapless brothers h been. He held his breath and in his fingers he clutched tightly the little toy canoe.

At first, the water was dazzling green in his eyes; then murky green; then tawny yellow; then black, and when it was black he felt as if the weight of it would force his heart up into his throat. There was a thundering drumming in his ears and then all at once he could feel nothing at all.

Sketco came to his senses as if he were waking from a deep slumber, to find himself floating on top of the sea in the brilliant daylight. He was clinging to his toy canoe. It had grown to the size of a little basket, and when the Raven saw this he grasped it more firmly and trod water while he threw his head back and shook the brine out of his eyes. As he grasped the canoe, it lengthened, and while he was in the act of climbing into it, it extended itself yet again.

Sketco laughed and stretched out his arms, for he had no paddle. The canoe leapt out of the sea and soared into the air like a beautiful white bird. Sketco laughed again when he saw his uncle scooting home across the ocean. His uncle heard the laugh and looked up at the sky, but the sun was in his eyes and all he could see was a white

Sketco landed on the beach and as soon as the canoe

touched the sand it shrank to its old size again. Sketco had lost his blanket in the sea, and as he ran naked into the village, he held the magical canoe tightly in his little brown fist.

The mother wept with joy to see her little son safe home and she clasped him in a tight embrace when he told her how the wicked uncle had tried to murder him.

"But I escaped him by my magic," he boasted. "Do not weep for my poor brothers," he said. "I will find them and restore them to you. And I will make my uncle pay for the evil he has brought upon us!"

"Hush!" the mother whispered. "Here he comes!"

Sketco ran to hide as the uncle stalked in, his face as black as a storm.

"Where is Sketco?" demanded the mother, trembling to realize that her brother was indeed a murderer, and afraid to trifle with him. "Tell me, what have you done with him?"

"I have done nothing with him," answered the scowling uncle. "He was like all the others. Pah!" He spat on the ground. "Your sons have brought me nothing but bad luck."

"What have you brought me?" the mother cried. "What have you brought me? You have drowned my sons!"

"Your sons were never meant for the sea. I have done my best to train them. They should have burrowed like rabbits on shore," he sneered, and turned to go.

"Did you catch any fish without me, Uncle?" asked Sketco, appearing coolly, as if nothing had happened.

The uncle turned pale and stood staring at the boy. Sketco walked up to him and touched his hand. The uncle started back as if he had been burnt; he shuddered; his eyes glared with fright and his teeth chattered.

"Where are my brothers?"

As the boy approached him, the uncle shrank to the ground and turned his face away.

Sketco leaned over him and shook his shoulder. The man shrank until he looked as if he had been struck down and broken. Suddenly he shrieked, kicked out at the boy, sprang up and dashed out of the house.

Sketco, who had dodged the blow of the man's foot, ran after him and reached the sand just in time to see his uncle hastening out to sea in his swift canoe.

The Raven turned back and said to his mother: "He has escaped. His magic is great, but mine is greater. I will go out into the world to search for him."

CHAPTER 4

THE RAVEN AND THE SHARKS

"Give me a little meat, Mother, and a little fish and some oil," said Sketco. "I am going abroad into the world to search out my uncle."

The mother grieved. "You were returned safe to me from the sea," she said sadly, "and must I lose you after all?"

"Have no fear, Mother," the Raven laughed. "I will come back again when I have avenged my brothers. And I will bring my brothers with me."

So she gave him meat and fish and oil, and he went down to the sea and launched his toy canoe. As it touched the water, it grew larger and larger, and a more graceful or proud canoe never glided over the waves.

When the mother saw the magical canoe, her heart lightened and she bade goodbye to her son cheerfully and watched him skim across the water and vanish out of sight.

Sketco flew toward the rocky island where the Gull People lived and when he came close to them he stood up in his canoe and shouted: "Gull People, have you seen my uncle pass this way?" The gulls beat about the sky restlessly, as if they were searching for something they would never find, and wailing and screaming because they could not find it.

"We have seen a man flying in a canoe," one of them answered mournfully. "He flew past the island faster than the wind runs."

"Which way? Which way?" asked Sketco, with his paddle poised in the air ready to cut into the sea and send himself spurting forward.

"To the West," the gull answered. "You will never catch him."

Sketco did not wait to hear more. He was out of sight before the gull had finished speaking, and the bird beat his wings and complained peevishly. Sketco coursed on until he was far beyond the place where the uncle had cast him into the sea.

Suddenly a shark put his head up out of the water and in his surprise Sketco nearly overturned the canoe.

But he quickly recovered and said: "Have you seen my uncle pass this way?"

"Is your uncle a man with a sharp spear?" asked the shark, staring at Sketco with a cold sinister eye.

"He is!" said Sketco. "You have seen him! Tell me where he is!"

Without answering, the shark dived under the water, turned, and tore a great gaping rent in the canoe with his keen pointed teeth.

The canoe quickly filled with water and sank almost before Sketco realized what had happened.

Once again, he saw the water green and yellow and black; once again, he felt the mass of the water crushing his ribs; once again, his ears were bursting with the throbbing of his stifling heart; and then he knew nothing.

When Sketco came to his senses this time, it was not to find himself floating on top of the water in the sunlight with his fingers holding tight to the magical canoe. He was lying on the sand at the bottom of the sea.

Slowly he lifted his head, painfully raised himself on his elbow. His head ached and his ears hummed, but the weight had been lifted from his body and he was surprised to know that he could breathe. He sat up and stared about him. As his eyes adjusted to the dim green light, he could make out the jagged rocks jutting out of the sand; and long, slowly waving dark curtains of weeds that shut him into a little room; and strange plants with stringy stalks and ragged leaves, plants without colour, that rose and fell and swayed and tugged as if they were obscene animals reaching out to lick him with tongues; and starfish, and great shells like open mouths, and clusters of small shells lying on the sandy floor in a profuse litter. A shadowy form that he thought was a smooth rock suddenly opened a glassy eye on him and sent out long feelers to reach for his body. He shuddered and realized that the water lay cold along his arms and on his shoulders and cold on his back and his chest and that the cold came up from the sand through his legs. He stood erect and found himself teetering on his toes, half floating, half carried away by the water. He walked and the water seemed at once to push him forward and to hinder him; he swam rather than walked, never touching the sand with his heels and using his hands to pull the weeds aside. "If I kick," thought Sketco, "I will shoot up through the water to the air again." He tried it but he floated up only a few feet and was forced down again by the pressure.

Sketco parted the slimy curtain with both hands and came full upon a space that stretched out wide and clear on every hand. Free from rocks and weeds and shells and litter, the sand stretched out level and smooth and white, almost gleaming, for here the sea ran clear up to the sun and the sun's rays poured down into it, mingling warm light with the water. A fish with a long horn and immense eyes swam sluggishly toward the boy and vanished with a flick of his tail when Sketco raised his hand; a hundred little fish, glowing with a strange light, swimming so close together that they seemed to be knit into a living curtain, hung before his eyes for a moment and disappeared without a sound.

Wading along, Sketco craned his neck and thrust his head back, but he could see nothing but green water all around him and above him, as boundless as the sky. He looked down again and then recoiled sharply, for there, in front of him, a few yards away, sat a circle of men with solemn faces. Like himself, they were naked, but about their waists they wore girdles of kelp and necklaces of tiny shells were strung round their throats. In their midst, prostrate on the sand, lay another man. A spear was sticking in his side.

As Sketco stood gaping, the Chief, who sat in the centre of the circle, raised his right arm and pointed a long finger at him. One of the shark men strode out, and, seizing Sketco with rough hands, dragged him forward and threw him on his knees.

"Is this the man," asked the Chief, "who murdered my son?"

"No!" Sketco cried.

"You look young and small to wield such a great spear," said the Chief of the Shark People.

Sketco half rose and looked boldly into the shark man's eyes. "I have more strength to pull out spears than to thrust them in," he said.

The men in the circle muttered but the Chief lifted his hand and they were silent.

"I think it was my uncle who murdered your son," said Sketco. "I am seeking him to avenge the death of my three brothers, whom he drowned."

"He asked me," said one of the shark men, "if I had seen his uncle. When I answered: 'Does your uncle carry a spear?' he said 'Yes' and I forthwith ripped his canoe open and brought him here."

"My uncle is a murderer," said Sketco, looking down at the body of the young man. He stood up. "I am a shaman," he said. One of the men moved to seize him but the Chief raised his hand and he stepped back again. "Let me heal your son, Chief of the Shark People."

The Chief looked at him and said nothing, so Sketco leaned over the dead youth and took hold of the shaft of the spear. He pulled it slightly and the youth stirred and groaned.

"Ah!" cried the Shark Chief. "He lives!" And all the men nodded their heads and murmured to one another.

Sketco sank back on his haunches and looked at the Chief. "Yes, I can cure him," he said, but he made no other move.

"Heal him, and you shall be free," promised the Shark Chief. "We will give you great riches. Precious abalone, and strange things from far away, corals, pink, delicate corals, and twisted shells, fluted shells, and limpid pearls, such things as we see in our travels . . ."

Sketco squatted and looked into the Chief's eyes. He felt now that he had power over the Shark People and that he need not fear them. "I know nothing of these things," he said.

"We will give you rich food in abundance, vegetables and fruits from the bottom of the sea, shellfish, jellies, delicate, strange things to eat . . ."

"My canoe is torn and sunk," said Sketco. "How can I reach home? Or how can I continue my quest?"

"I will give you a shark dress," said the Chief, "and you may swim swiftly to your home. If you will, you may range the seas as a shark until you find your uncle and kill him."

Sketco bent once more over the Chief's son and tugged at the spear. It came easily out of his side and the blood flowed after it, clouding the water murkily. But Sketco put his hand on the wound, and the bleeding was staunched. When he took his hand away, there was not even a scar to be seen, and the young shark man rose up as from a sleep, yawning and lifting his arms and stretching his legs. All the Shark People crowded round him, feeling his side and asking him questions until he was bewildered.

"You have done a good thing," said the Chief to Sketco. "I do not understand how one so young should be such a powerful shaman. Stay with us, and when you are old enough you shall marry my daughter."

Sketco shook his head.

"You shall be honoured forever among the People of the Sea. You shall be Chief when I am dead."

Sketco thanked him and said: "No, I have other work to do."

The Chief bowed gravely and ordered one of the men to bring a shark dress for him.

"Let us all swim with the young shaman," said the Chief, "and see him safely on his journey."

So Sketco put on his shark dress, which fitted completely over his small body and gave him a sharp nose and a mouth full of sharp teeth, and keen eyes. He did not feel like himself with this new head, and he missed the use of his arms and legs, which were held fast, but he took a joy in the lithe body, the brisk fins and the long sturdy tail, and he swam with great gusto.

"You were meant to be a shark," the Chief said to him in a flattering voice as they swam side by side. "Stay with us."

But Sketco merely grinned with his white shark's teeth, and they climbed up the steep water to the sunlight.

"A shark! Never!" Sketco thought when he put his nose above the water and caught sight of the sun swimming among the clouds that were tumbled over the wide blue sky. He thought of the dank weeds licking the water in the depths of the sea and writhing along the ooze and the sand; of the silent, goggle-eyed fish; he thought of the kelp clinging damply to the bodies of the Shark People; and of the dimness and coldness of their world, and he struck out toward the shore. He could see a faint smudge of green and, below it, patches of white against which the waves were breaking. He rejoiced and said: "I will make another canoe! How much better it is to be on top of the water than underneath it!"

Suddenly Sketco remembered his brothers and he

turned to the Shark Chief and said: "Have you seen my drowned brothers in your travels?"

"I was afraid you had forgotten your brothers," said the Shark Chief cunningly.

"Then you have seen them?"

The Shark Chief lied, for he wished to have Sketco stay with him as a shaman, to heal the hurts of the Shark People with his magic. "I know where they are," he said glibly.

"Will you take me to them?"

"Well," said the Chief doubtfully, "it is not a simple matter. You see, they are sheltered by a rock which is not easy to find. If you promise to remain with the Shark People, I will lead you to the place."

"I saved the life of your son!" cried Sketco. "You promised me untold riches . . ."

"You would not have them."

"I am asking a small thing . . ." But before Sketco could finish his protest there was a loud commotion and splashing and the Chief and all the other sharks disappeared in a twinkling.

Sketco turned in bewilderment, half inclined to think that they had suddenly deserted him, half impelled to dive after them, and at the same time darting around to see if some urgent danger threatened. He caught sight of a boat almost riding over him and he dived in a panic. At the same instant, something struck him and shook him violently. He caught his breath and dived deeper. As he did so, he felt a violent pain which abruptly ceased and left him senseless.

CHAPTER 5

THE THUNDER MAN

Sketco had been speared by a fisherman, but he did not know what had happened. He did not know that the giant Thunder Man had pierced him and that he reached out into the water and grasped him by the tail.

"That's a small fellow," rumbled the Thunder Man, throwing Sketco into the bottom of the canoe with a thud. He turned to his daughter, who was steering. "But he's a nice sleek one, isn't he? See how silvery his belly is!" He laughed with a great roar, because his daughter blushed. "He must have been young and foolish!" bellowed the Thunder Man. "All the other lads got away quickly enough. Well, with the whales, this will be enough for one day. He will make a dainty morsel for your breakfast."

"It seems a pity to kill him," said the girl sadly.

"Come, you soft-hearted fool! You can't go falling in love with every fish we catch!" shouted the Thunder Man, thrusting his paddle into the water.

"I am not in love with him," said the girl, blushing again. "But he seems different from the other sharks. He has a gentle look."

"If we pity everything we kill," said the Thunder Man, puffing and blowing, "you'll never eat. Then we'll have to be pitying *you.*"

The girl said no more until they beached the canoe. Then she said: "If you take the whales, I will carry the shark."

The Thunder Man winked at her and hoisted two huge whales up on his back. He staggered off with them, grasping them by the tails with great fists, one over each shoulder. As if to forestall her father's raillery, the girl took hold of the shark by the tail and swung it carelessly as she walked.

Together the giant and his giant daughter plodded across the sand and trudged up the long steep trail into the mountains. Now and again, the Thunder Man paused and crouched to shift his burden for greater comfort, but the girl did not find Sketco heavy.

The trail was narrow and rough, almost hidden among the broken rocks and choked with ferns and berry bushes, but the giant and his daughter took long strides, crossing tumbling torrents with one step, as if they were no more than trickles of water, and crushing saplings under their heels as easily as if they were stepping on fireweed. Up they went through the sloping woods, stopping neither for deadfall nor thicket, nor looking behind at the sea that glimmered far below them. They scrambled up high rock benches that were no more than stairs to their legs and heedlessly tracked through a beautiful alpine meadow that was overrun with forget-me-nots and columbines and fireweed and paintbrush. Then they turned and walked along a ridge, and so into a bog and beyond that to where the trees were stunted and where the furze was springy under their feet. Higher they climbed and higher, until there seemed to be no more life, nothing but dead grey rock encrusted with dull grey-green lichens, and great slides of grey shale that shifted under their tread, and boulders with snow patches lying in their shadows. It was as if a terrible fire had stormed through the mountain pass, sucking the life out of every creature and leaving nothing but the dry bones. Even the snow was tinged with brown, as if it had been scorched. A stream, which had gushed out of the earth too late to quench the great fire, went roaring down to the valley. Marmots whistled shrilly against the noise of water and wind, as they scuttled among the rocks and the heaps of cinders and sat up on their hind legs to watch with suspicious eyes the tramping giants.

But Thunder and his daughter paid no heed to any of these things. He with his whales on his back and she swinging Sketco, they toiled up and up until they were hobbling across the moraine of a glacier that poured down the mountainside like a river of crushed rock and gravel. Then they climbed up the glacier itself. The ice was coated with sand but it was pitted with holes dug by the sun and each little cup was brimming with water. The water, clear blue and cold, trickled over the ice with a tinkling sound and gushed out of crevasses, to pour into a torrent that ran from under the ice and down through the gravel and the purple fireweed to the wild brook. Thunder Man had cut steps in the glacier and, slippery as it was, in spite of the sand, the climb was not hard for the great crunching feet of the giants.

Through another desolation of tumbled rock they climbed and into the everlasting snow. So deep were their footprints in the white snow that a man could have fallen in, but no man had ever ventured up as high as the house of the Thunder Man.

With his daughter, Lightning, Thunder Man lived in an enormous house built of great slabs of granite. It stood on the peak of a high mountain, exposed to all the winds of heaven, but there was no wind strong enough to shake it and the heaviest snows could never bear it down. The snow was banked around it on three sides, all but the one in which the door hung, and there were no windows. The door was a single slab of stone, so balanced that it opened to the Thunder Man's slightest touch, but it closed so quickly that a stranger would have been crushed to death as he tried to enter the giant's house. It shut with a crash of thunder that made the mountain shake to its foundations, and the people in the valleys below or out on the sea would look up and say: "Thunder Man is shutting his door."

Within, the house was like a massive square cave, so high that a bird might have grown weary in his flight before he reached the ceiling and so wide that many Indian villages might have camped side by side on its floor. It was darker than night, for night at least has its stars, but the stone walls were thickly coated with frost and the white frost gave a faint glow which was light enough for the sharp eyes of Thunder and his daughter.

"Let us set to work to smoke our fish," said Thunder Man, as they entered. He let the two whales slide off his back to the floor and stood stretching his arms and shrugging his shoulders.

Lightning dropped the shark and disappeared into a corner of the house to build up a great fire. When she returned, she found her father busy cutting the whales into strips. He tossed her a knife and she knelt down and bent over the shark. She hesitated, but her father laughed at her, so she blushed and thrust the point of the knife into the shark's throat. She slit him down the middle, revealing young Sketco, who lay within the shark skin as if he were fast asleep.

Lightning gasped with astonishment and drew back, letting the knife fall from her hand.

"What is it?" boomed the Thunder Man, looking up from his blubber.

"The shark!" the girl cried. "It is a young man!" Thunder Man rubbed the sweat off his face with the back of his hand and rose to look.

"So this is why you were so careful of him!" he laughed. He picked up the shark carcass and dug Sketco out with his fingers.

"Is he dead?" asked Lightning, holding her breath and staring at the boy with wide open eyes.

Thunder Man squeezed Sketco's chest with his thumb. He felt the heart beat under the pressure. "He is alive. Look, the colour is coming back into his cheeks and his body is tightening."

He set Sketco down on the floor. Feeling the life returning to his body, the boy stretched and winced. He groaned and opened his eyes but he saw nothing and he was too weak to remember anything, so he sank down, shivered a little with the cold and fell asleep.

"Has he died again?" asked Lightning.

"No," her father replied. "He is sleeping. The poor boy is cold," he added. "Cover him up."

"I will carry him to the fire." The girl lifted Sketco gently and sat beside the fire, warming him with the palms of her hands, stroking him as if he were a little kitten, and bathing the wound she discovered in his breast. It was not a serious wound, because the fish spear had just grazed him, burying its point in the fat that lay underneath the skin of the shark dress. Thunder Man went on cutting up the whale meat, and he gave Lightning a sliver, which she held to Sketco's mouth. The boy was hungry and, like an infant, he sucked it greedily without waking.

When at last he did wake, he struggled in the girl's hands and wondered where he was. He could not understand the darkness and the smell of smoke and drying whale flesh, and when he sat up and saw the glare of the fire, he was frightened. The grasp of Lightning's warm fingers bewildered him still more and he cried out:

"Where am I? What has become of me?"

"Hush!" soothed the girl. "You are in Thunder Man's house. You need not be alarmed."

Sketco cried: "I can't see! Let me see! Let me see!"

"Are you afraid of the dark?" rumbled the voice of the Thunder Man. He set fire to a great pan of oil.

The flaring light revealed only a small space of the great stone house and it sent terrible shadows shuddering into all the corners, but Sketco could see Thunder Man and his daughter towering above him and his heart stood still. But Sketco was full of courage. He slipped down from Lightning's knee, falling heavily; but he regained his feet and stood on the floor with his hands on his hips and his legs apart, facing the giants impudently.

"What a tall fellow you are!" he said to the Thunder Man. "Is it you who makes all the noise?"

Lightning laughed and Thunder Man scowled, but with good nature.

"You naked little coney," he said. "One flick of my hand and where do you think you would be?"

"Where am I now?" asked Sketco boldly.

"You are in my house!" bellowed the Thunder Man, "and keep a civil tongue in your head while you are in it, you slippery little minnow!"

Sketco knitted his brows. "I was swimming with the sharks," he remembered. "Oh, you speared me, and brought me here! You thought I was a shark!"

"My daughter brought you here." He screwed his face into a grin. "She gets lonely up here and you will make a lively plaything for her. When you grow up, you may marry her." He guffawed.

"I have work to do," said Sketco, as the girl bent her head and blushed. "I am Sketco, the Raven, and I am out in the world in search of my uncle who murdered my three brothers and tried to murder me. Have you seen my uncle in your travels over the mountains?"

"Is he any bigger than you?" asked the Thunder Man derisively.

"He has magic," said Sketco, thrusting out his chin impudently. "And so have I!"

"Oh, have you? Let us see you turn a somersault then!"

"Father, do not tease the poor little fellow!" implored Lightning.

But Sketco smiled and turned a somersault and while the Thunder Man was shaking his sides laughing at him, he ran suddenly and nimbly behind him, put his shoulder to the giant's heel and pushed with all his strength.

The Thunder Man lost his balance, slipped and fell on his rump with a crash that made the house rattle, while Sketco skipped quickly between his legs.

Lightning laughed at her father's discomfiture. The giant roared, but he was not angry. "You have very powerful magic," he said, laughing until the tears stood in his eyes. "You must stay with us and help us."

"Gladly," said the Raven cunningly, "but I cannot see in the dark."

"Oh, is that all?" asked Thunder. He leaned forward and suddenly caught the wriggling Sketco by one leg. His daughter rose and scratched some frost off the wall with her fingernail. She anointed Sketco's eyes with the frost and he squirmed, because it made them smart, but when he blinked and opened them again he found that he could see as well as if the great cave were flooded with sunlight.

"That is my magic," said the Thunder Man, releasing him. He turned away and picked up his knife. "Now I have work to do. And besides, I am too old for play." He went back to his task of cutting up the whales.

"Are you cold?" Lightning asked Sketco, looking down at his trembling little body.

"No," the boy lied. But he shuddered violently, both

with cold and because he feared the giants, kindly as they seemed, and the vastness of their house terrified him.

Lightning smiled, cut off a small corner of her blanket and wrapped him in its folds. "Now you will be warm, little fish," she said. "Sit by the fire. I must go out and get some more wood."

She returned with an armful of tree trunks and made such a blaze that Sketco could not stand the heat. "If I stay here," he thought, "I shall die, either from the heat or the cold." Even if he escaped both, he could not bear the thought of being shut up for the rest of his life with these giants on the mountain top. As if she had read his thoughts, Lightning said: "There is no use your trying to escape, little playmate, because, small as you are, the great door will slam and crush you to a bloodstain. It fits very snugly."

There was only this one door to the house and there were no windows. The only way out then was the smoke-hole, far up in a corner of the roof. Small Sketco stood as close to the fire as he dared, stretching his head back as far as it would go, and watched the smoke drift up. He could not see the hole, for at the top, miles upward, it seemed, the smoke hung like a murky cloud. Sketco sighed. "If only I could change myself into a spark!" he wished. But he was young and his magic was not yet strong enough for such feats. "If I had my knife," he said to himself, "I could carve myself a bird out of one of Lightning's sticks and sail up on the smoke." But his knife, like his enchanted canoe, was lost.

"My father has decided to make a storm," said Thunder Man's daughter one day.

"Why?" asked Sketco.

"Why? What a stupid question! I never saw such a silly child! Why!"

"I know I am stupid," said the Raven," but I have not seen much of the world. I have seen your father thundering across the sky and I have seen the flash of your wings, but why do you make storms?"

"Because we have always made them," retorted Lightning. "Now you must remain here and be a good boy."

"Let me come with you!" pleaded Sketco.

"No. You are too small. You will only get hurt."

The great rumbling voice of her father was heard: "Are you ready, Lightning?"

"Ready, Father," Lightning answered, darting a look at Sketco. She twisted her body quickly, craned her neck, stretched her arms above her head; and there she stood, transformed into a beautiful bird, tremendous, but graceful and feathered in glittering silver. As she raised her wings, the lightning flashed from under them, violet and red, so piercing that Sketco staggered back and pressed his hands to his eyes. When he looked up, he saw Thunder Man standing before him, in the shape of a bird so gigantic and black that Sketco trembled and thought of the great thunderclouds he had so often seen rolling over the sky in the heat of summer.

"Well, little minnow," said the Thunder Man jovially, "what are you frightened of? You must be brave, because we are leaving the house in your care. Don't let anyone in to steal our blubber." He laughed with a loud voice and clapped his wings thunderously. "And don't eat all the whale yourself!" He roared again, spread his vast wings and sailed out through the door, with Lightning close behind him. Sketco hung back a moment, then he ran after them, but the door slammed in his face and the shock sent him spinning across the floor.

Sketco sat on the ground for a long time, screwing up his face and scratching his head. "I must get out!" he exclaimed, jumping to his feet and pacing up and down. "I must get out! I cannot stay here all my life, shut away from the world. I must find my uncle." He clenched his little fists and stamped his feet on the stone flagging.

"I must avenge my brothers."

He ran over to the wall, peered closely at it and tried it with his fingers. It was so cold that it stung. It was smoothly varnished with frost and there was no toehold anywhere.

Sketco turned away in despair. He ran to the corner where the Thunder Man's tools lay, but the knives were nearly as big as he was. Frantically he searched among the possessions of the giant and his daughter. He found a string of beads that Lightning sometimes wore round her neck and had thrown in the corner because the thread was broken. With a cry of delight, Sketco seized hold of one of the beads with both hands and dragged it off the string. Then he ran to the fuel heap and brought back a splinter of wood, which he fitted into the hole in the bead. Thus he made himself a sledge-hammer and he jumped up and down with glee at his cleverness.

The boy hoisted the hammer on his shoulder and marched over to the wall nearest the fire. Exerting all his energy, he began his attack on the frost crust. At first, he was wobbly in his stroke, but as he struck, he fell into a rhythm, and, sweating from every pore, he swung steadily and surely from the hips, bringing back and shoulders into the work.

When he had cut the first hole deep enough so that it

would give him a good grip for his toes, he dropped the hammer and let his aching arms fall slack at his sides. He had hardly strength enough to wipe the sweat out of his eyes. But he did not rest long, for he was afraid that the Thunder Man would come back and discover that he was trying to escape. He cut another step in the wall and then he suddenly realized that he could not go on. He could not reach any higher and it would be impossible for him to cling to the vertical wall and wield the hammer.

Sketco sank down and wept in his disappointment. He looked up at the roof of the house, dim in the distance, and cried bitterly. But nothing is done by crying, and the boy soon thought of a new idea. He wrenched the bead from its handle and, taking hold of it in both hands, went to the wall and put his foot in the first hole he had cut. Clinging with his knees and elbows, and his bare body almost sticking to the frost, he edged up to the second hole and with the greatest difficulty began chipping away the ice above. It was desperately slow work, because he was afraid to do more than scrape with the bead, lest he should lose his balance and fall. As it was, his warm flesh began to stick to the wall. It held him on his perch, but he was afraid that his skin would be torn when he moved.

Sketco, suffering agonies from cramp and cold, was

still nibbling away at the frost to make his third toehold when Thunder Man stalked in.

"Aha!" he cried. "Trying to pick my house to pieces, are you!"

In his fright, Sketco dropped the bead and would have fallen like a dead fly from the wall had not the giant seized him.

"What do you think of this?" said the giant, holding out Sketco's quivering body to his daughter. "He was trying to dig his way out with one of your beads for an axe."

"Oh, poor child, he is all raw and bleeding from the frost!" cried the girl. "Let me have him." She took the boy tenderly and spoke soothingly to him. Poor Sketco, cold and sore and aching in every fibre, was relieved that he had been caught, in spite of his bitter disappointment, and he allowed Lightning to rub healing salve on his hurts.

"Well," said Thunder Man, standing, watching, with his hands on his hips, "the youngster has pluck. If we hadn't come in, he would have fallen and broken his little bones, or he would have frozen to death. It's a long way up, my boy, for a mite like you. It would have taken you years, at your rate of going, and once you were high enough, you'd have had to keep moving up unless you wanted to fall down and kill yourself. But of course you would have perished of starvation. Where is your magic now?" He laughed and poked at Sketco playfully with his enormous forefinger. The boy bit his lip and turned his head away to hide the tears.

"Cheer up!" shouted the Thunder Man. "Tell him about the fine storm we had, Lightning. I have to get some wood. It's going to be a cold night up here."

As his body healed and he got back the strength of his arms, Sketco began to scheme again in his mind, because he had a heart that was young and strong and full of hope. He said nothing, however, and the giants thought that he had decided to be content with them.

The day came when they went out to make another storm, leaving Sketco behind them and warning him against another foolish attempt to escape. When the boy heard the great stone door shut behind them, he gritted his teeth in anger.

"Oh," he cried, "if only I could fly!" He lifted himself on his toes and stretched out his arms. "I am a raven, why should I not have wings?"

He strained his neck, flung his arms out and thrust his little chest forward. He raised himself on his toes again and stretched with all his might. At that moment, he was transformed into a bird, feathered all over, from crown to heel, in dusky red, the colour of his own skin. His heart pumped excitedly under the feathers of his breast and he shouted with joy, running about the room and flapping his wings and spreading out his tail, when suddenly he found himself floating in the air.

Sketco flew to the door but it was shut fast and it would not open to the touch of his wings. Then he circled the vast room and spiralled upward. The smoke-hole was the only way out. He soared. Up, up he flew, until his young wings were weary. The fire, at first rising up in such a heat that he was almost scorched, was sunk far below, like a small spark glowing red in the gloom, but the smoke filled his eyes and made them water, and he began to feel dizzy as well as weary. For a moment, he shut his aching eyes and allowed his wings to sag. As if he had crumpled, he lurched and began to fall. Down, down, down, down. His head was spinning, he was almost senseless, he did not know what was happening to him.

Suddenly he came to himself and in a panic quickly struck out. He forced his aching wings to carry him up again, higher, higher. In his dread, he thought he could hear the beating of the Thunder Man's black pinions beneath him. It was his own heart pulsing in his ears, but he did not know, and he strained every muscle and nerve.

Above his head, a patch of light appeared, growing larger and brighter as he ascended, and at last he burst through the hole as if he had been shot out.

For a moment, Sketco wavered weakly and nearly fell back into the house, but he managed to reel away and he sank exhausted on a peak of snow which was heaped on the roof. He closed his eyes and lay in a miserable huddle, as if he had been badly buffeted and beaten. But he soon stirred himself, as he began to get his breath again, for he was afraid that Thunder and Lightning would discover him.

As he spread his wings and rose from the roof, Sketco saw that the imprint of his body on the snow was black. He was puzzled, for the snow was far from the smoke-hole and it was freshly fallen, the purest white. He looked at his broad wings and saw that they were no longer dusky red but black. The soot had clung to him as he flew up through the smoke. Now he shook his wings and ruffled all his feathers. Flakes of soot fell on the snow, but Sketco remained black, and from that day to this the Raven's feathers have never changed their colour.

CHAPTER 6

THE LONELY HOUSE

As Sketco sailed up into the blue sky, revelling in his freedom and in the rhythm of his wings, ever growing stronger, he looked down at the earth below him. The glistening mountain peaks lay like snowy islands in a great billowing sea of clouds, and weaving their way in and out of the clouds, swiftly flying back and forth, he could see the Thunder Bird and his daughter Lightning. Although he could hear the thunder but faintly, he could see the lightning flashing out from beneath the daughter's wings, as she beat across the foaming sky, and cutting downward violently. How the clouds rolled and churned! Hanging on his wings, Sketco watched, fascinated, forgetting to be frightened.

At length, Thunder and Lightning flew close together and seemed to speak to one another. They soared above the cloud-wrack and Sketco saw them fly back toward their mountain and disappear. The heavy clouds shifted and collapsed, broke apart and drifted away from one another, finally vanishing completely. The sun poured down into the valleys and revealed to the Raven's sharp eyes width after width of green, and many a glistening river and shining spread of lake, and many a white-frothing cascade and, leagues away, the splendid ocean.

As if to wake himself out of a dream, Sketco shook himself, dipped his wings into the air and set off in the direction of the sea.

Down, down he dropped, as he spied the rocks up-thrust in a jagged line along the shore; down, with the swiftness of the wind, until his feet touched the ground. When he folded his wings, they turned into arms, his feathers vanished, and he was once more a small boy. He was grimy from soot and smoke, so he waded into a pool that gleamed among the rocks and washed himself until he was clean and shining dusky red again. Then he climbed up on a high rock and sat down in the sun to dry, prying off shellfish with his fingers and eating them greedily, for he was ravenous with hunger.

"Thunder Man will never catch me now," said Sketco to himself, as he stood up and stretched. "I am too clever for him, even if he is a mighty giant." He brandished his hands impudently. "But I must be clever enough to catch my uncle," he added soberly.

He slipped down off the rock and curled up in a little sandy nook in the sun and fell fast asleep. A crab scuttled out and tickled his toes, and a flock of gulls dropped out of the sky to see what it was that lay there; they quarrelled noisily among themselves, chasing one another away so that each could have a better look; but Sketco slept soundly.

When Sketco wakened, he sat up and stretched and rubbed his eyes. He had slept long and for a moment could not remember where he was. He saw that he was sitting on a little patch of sand hemmed in by the rocks and he could hear the beat and wash of the sea. As if they were dreams, he began to remember the giant Thunder Man and his daughter Lightning and their dreadful cold house on top of the mountain peak; and then the sharks came back to his mind; the dim, overhanging water, the waving curtains of weeds and the scuttling jelly-fish. The boy shuddered and stood up. Picking his way carefully, because the sharp rocks cut his feet, he clambered up a tall stone and stood on top, gazing out over the sea.

The heaving ocean sprawled under the vast blue sky and both sea and sky were shimmering with light as if the sky poured it into the sea and the sea poured it back into the sky again so rapidly that they were both continually awash with light and never for a moment cold. The sun, it seemed to Sketco, was tossed from sea to sky like a golden ball. As if they were not sure whether they belonged to sky or sea, the gulls ranged restlessly backward and forward, up and down, round and round, endlessly searching, never finding, lighting a moment on the gleaming water, but never at peace.

"Gull People! Gull People!" called Sketco, standing on his rock and putting his hand to his mouth.

Four gulls heard him and circled about his head.

"What are you shouting for, Indian boy?" asked one of them querulously.

"Have you seen my uncle?" asked Sketco.

"We have seen the Thunder beat his way across the sky," said the second gull.

"The Thunder is not my uncle," said Sketco quickly.

"We have seen the Whale spitting higher than a great chief can spit," the third said.

"My uncle is not a great chief and he cannot spout like the Whale; but he can make the Whale spout blood," said Sketco.

"Your uncle is a great killer?" the fourth gull asked.

"He murdered my three brothers. But they were only children."

"You must ask your murdered brothers where your uncle is."

"You must go down to them in the land of the dead."

Sketco asked: "Where do the dead dwell?"

"That, we cannot tell you," said the first gull.

"It is beyond the shadows," said the second.

"More we know not," said the third.

The fourth said: "No one ever tells us anything."

They wheeled and flew away, leaving the boy standing on the rock, a little puzzled, and a little angry with the gulls for their complaining voices.

He stood a long time, watching their white wings and looking out over the sea, and at last he slipped down from the rock and picked his way along the beach. A dead cod was washed up at his feet and Sketco stopped to speak to it.

"Where do you come from?" he asked.

The water pushed the dead fish toward him and drew it back again.

"Where is the land of the dead?" Sketco asked.

A heavy wave threw the fish up on the sand and left it lying there with its mouth pointing inland.

"Thank you, Cod Man," said Sketco and, turning his back on the ocean, he pushed on toward the forest.

He stumbled along, footsore and hungry and, just as he was about to fall from weariness, he came upon a dead owl sprawling on the ground with its white feathers strewn about the carpet of pine needles like new snow.

Leaning over it, Sketco said: "Owl Man, in your quiet flight, have you seen my brothers?"

As he spoke, the wind picked up a handful of feathers and carried them lightly along the air in front of the boy.

Sketco followed eagerly. But his heart sank as one by one the feathers drifted to the ground or settled on the branches of the trees.

Weary and disappointed, he crouched down under a lofty cedar. The trees stood in the gloom of their own shadows. The darkness seemed to rise from the ground and creep up to the sky.

"Shadow People," pleaded Sketco, "tell me where you have hidden my brothers!"

The trees rustled, but Sketco could not understand their words, and the shadows gathered thicker and said nothing.

Closer and closer, the shadows of the forest gathered round his small body. Gently they lifted him in their arms and softly they carried him away, but he knew nothing, for he was sound asleep.

When the young Raven awakened, he did not know where he was, and he had forgotten about his brothers. He was conscious of nothing but legs and arms that were stiff with cold and of a great gnawing pain in his belly. Painfully he stretched himself and began to search for food. He discovered a few berries but they made him only the hungrier. Hearing the sound of water, he scrambled through the bush until he reached the river.

Scratched and torn and bleeding, Sketco struggled down into the canyon and stood on a little strip of pebbles past which the water raced and roared, fighting and foaming in a white lather. For a moment he stood with his hands on his hips, getting back his breath and watching the salmon leaping up the stream.

Then he thrust out his stomach and shouted mockingly: "You're a very fine jumper, Salmon Man, but you can't jump on my belly!"

One of the salmon promptly jumped out of the water and threw himself at the boy. So sudden and swift was the jump and so heavy the fish, that it knocked the wind out of Sketco and he was thrown on his back, senseless.

When he revived and managed to sit up, he saw the

salmon, with a ring of foam round his neck, laughing at him.

"It — was — a mighty — jump — Salmon Man," the Raven gasped. He tried to smile. "But you — couldn't — do it again!"

He was hardly on his feet when the salmon leapt out of the water and dealt him such a blow in the belly that he was again knocked down unconscious.

It was a long time before he opened his eyes and was able to breathe again, and it was a longer time before he sat up, for his stomach was not only empty but very sore.

But the Raven, as he went about the world, was learning to be crafty and as he lay gasping for breath and rubbing his belly with both hands, he made up his mind that his trick to catch the fish would work better the third time.

He rose, screwing his face with pain and doubling up in the middle, and then he rested on his knees and, putting one foot on the ground, slowly straightened himself.

The salmon grinned at him from the water.

"You think you are a clever little boy, do you?" he jeered.

"Perhaps you are more clever than I am," said Sketco. Every word hurt him, but he tried to smile.

"You invited me to butt you in the belly," said the salmon. "Shall I do it again, or shall I go on, up the river?"

"Watch me," said Sketco. "I will show you a trick." He went about gathering stones and building them into a little wall along the water's edge.

"What are you doing?" asked the salmon, and some of his friends crowded around him to see.

"I cannot jump like you," said Sketco, "but this is one thing I can do. I am building a corral."

"What is a corral?" asked the Salmon Man.

"You shall see," Sketco promised and went on building. At last he stood behind his little stone wall and said to the fish: "Now strike me in the belly!"

He thrust out his body and capered about derisively.

"Do you think I can't jump over those stones?" the salmon sneered. "Watch out, my boy! I'll knock the wind out of you this time so that it never comes back into your body!"

With a mighty spring, he leapt out of the river and over the wall. But he fell floundering on the pebbly sand, for Sketco dodged him just in time.

"Ha! Ha!" laughed Sketco. "You could jump over the wall, but you can't jump back!"

The fish had fallen so heavily that he was bruised and out of breath himself this time. He did not have the strength to jump again, and the wall prevented him from sliding back into the water.

"Why do you think I asked you to jump on me?" the boy asked, standing with legs apart and looking down at the gasping salmon. "Because I wanted to catch you," he laughed. "Twice, I was too slow, but now you shall go *into* my belly!"

"Be sure," gasped the fish, "to burn my bones when you have cooked me. Unless you do this, my soul will not return to my people."

"With pleasure," Sketco promised, and he hit the fish on the head with a stone.

With hunger driving him, Sketco lost no time scrambling up the bank and hurrying off to make a fire. It was hard work, because the salmon was heavy to drag.

When he came to a clearing in the woods, he gathered bark and moss and set it alight by rubbing two sticks together until they smoked and burst into flame. Then he roasted his fish and ate it greedily. But he remembered to put the bones on the fire so that the dead salmon should return to the Salmon People.

Dozing beside the fire after his feast, Sketco remembered his brothers, but he did not know that even now he was in the land of shadows, and he fell asleep before he thought any more.

When he woke up, it was nightfall, but he was not afraid, for the Lightning Woman had anointed his eyes so that he could see in the dark, and now he felt rested and refreshed and strong. What was left of the smouldering fire he stamped out with his bare feet so that no living sparks should be left to destroy the forest.

Striding along through the woods, the Raven came upon a lonely house. He stopped and listened, but he heard no sound of life and he saw no movement. He crept toward it cautiously and peered in through the doorway. In the centre of the floor lay the remains of a fire, still warm, and in their places about the house were fish harpoons with heads of bone, and baskets and mats, and salmon was drying on the racks overhead.

Sketco picked up one of the salmon spears and weighed it in his hand. He thought of the fish in the river. "This," he said to himself, "would be better than being smitten in the stomach!"

He strained his eyes and ears, looking and listening, but there was neither sight nor sound of living man.

"I will borrow the harpoon," said the Raven and,

picking it up, he was walking out of the house when something struck his leg.

"What was that?" he cried, turning quickly.

A stick lay on the ground at his feet, but there was nothing else to be seen.

"It must have fallen," he said, looking at the roof as he hastened out.

As he went, he felt another tap on his leg. He broke into a run when he was out of the house. But he was struck again and with such force this time that he stumbled and fell. His leg was broken.

Sketco cried from the pain, but surprise and fright stopped his tears when he felt strong, warm hands grasping his leg and squeezing it.

"Who are you?" he whispered. "I cannot see you. Speak to me!"

A voice answered him: "Why do you steal our spear?" Sketco trembled and burst out crying.

"I wanted to copy it and make one for myself," he said. "I would have brought it back to you."

"We will help you," answered the voice.

Still the Raven could see no one, but he was carried in strong arms back to the house and there set down on the ground.

"Your leg is better," said the voice, "but the Raven will always limp."

"Where are you?" Sketco asked, too bewildered to be worried about limping. "I cannot see anything. I did not see anyone, so I borrowed the spear to copy . . ."

"You cannot see the dead," said another voice.

"We are the ghosts," said the first voice that had spoken.

"Oh!" Sketco cried, "you can help me find my brothers!"

"We will help you," said the first voice. But the ghost was thinking of the spear. "I will give you half of my lower rib."

Sketco saw no movement and heard nothing, but in a moment he found a bone in his hands.

"When you sharpen it," said the voice, "it will turn into a spearhead. But you must use it only at night."

The Raven thanked him and then said: "While I have been thinking about my own hunger, I have forgotten my brothers and my uncle who murdered them. I must restore my brothers to their mother, for I have promised, and I must avenge their death. Are my brothers here? I cannot see any of you."

"Your brothers are not here," answered the voices.

"But, of course, the dead have many houses," said one.

"How did they die?" another asked.

"They were drowned."

"Then you must go to the island in the middle of the sea."

"Thank you," said the Raven. He hesitated. "How shall I find the island?" he asked.

"The Fog Man is the only person who could tell you," one of the ghosts replied.

"He keeps it hidden from the eyes of the living."

"He will not keep it hidden from me!" cried the Raven. "I will find a way to make him tell me!"

CHAPTER 7

SKETCO FINDS HIS BROTHERS

"You must go back through the land of the living to reach the ocean and the island of the drowned," they told him.

"I do not know how I came here," said Sketco. "The Cod Man told me to go inland, and the Wind and the owl's feathers led me into the forest. But I lost my way and there I fell asleep. When I woke up I did not remember anything except that I was hungry, and I caught the salmon by a trick, and then I found your house."

He felt that he was speaking to the air, for he could see no one, but the rib was in his hand and the voices of the ghosts answered him.

"You were brought here by the shadows, and with the shadows you must return."

A hand touched his hair and stroked his forehead. The fingers gently closed his eyes.

"Sleep, and when you wake you will be once again

among the living."

Sketco felt drowsy and soon he fell into slumber.

He awakened, to find himself lying on his back under the tall cedar. Although the woods were gloomy, he knew that it was daylight. Had he been dreaming? He thought of the salmon and rubbed his stomach. Then he remembered the Ghost People. When he saw the bone they had given him for a spearhead lying a few feet from where he had been sleeping, and when he limped as he ran to pick it up, he realized that he had not been dreaming.

"I must find the Fog Man," said Sketco, "and ask him to lead me to the island of the drowned."

"It may be a long way," he thought. Then he remembered that he could fly and laughed. Stretching up on his tiptoes, he transformed himself into the form of a bird, with the blackest of feathers in spite of his washing in the pool by the sea after he had escaped from the Thunder Man. Whenever Sketco appeared as a human being, it was always as an Indian, dusky red, but whenever he took on his Raven shape, he was as black as soot.

He seized the bone in his beak, spread his wings and flew up between the lofty trees, over their tops and far out toward the ocean.

When he came to a long beach, he alighted, and when

his feet touched the ground, he changed into his other shape. As he sauntered along the sand, swinging the rib in his hand and singing to himself, he approached an old man who sat at the edge of the water patching a canoe.

"Why don't you put your straw hat on, old man?" he asked impudently. The man's hat was lying on the beach beside the canoe. "The sun will scorch your hair."

"Why don't you keep your tongue in, child?" the old man returned, glaring at him. "A gull might snap it off."

"I am not a child," replied Sketco, who had indeed grown since he left home on his adventures.

The old man snorted and returned to his work.

"You are a very old man," said the Raven, more politely. "How old are you?"

"I have no time to count my years," said the old man curtly.

"I am old, too," boasted Sketco. "I have been in the country of the Ghosts and I have roamed the skies with the Thunder Man, and been with his daughter."

"You are old enough in lies," said the old man, without looking up.

"I have lived with the Shark People at the bottom of the sea," said Sketco. He squatted on his haunches and began drawing lines in the sand with his bone.

The old man grunted.

"How far back can you remember?" the boy asked. "I remember the days when the rocks were soft."

The old man rose, glowering at him, and began to push the canoe into the water. The Raven laughed.

"Where are you going, Kanugu?" he asked.

"Do you know my name?" The old man darted a look at him.

"I know many things."

"Then you know where I am going and I need not tell you."

He shoved the canoe into the water, tossed his straw hat in and leapt in after it.

Sketco jumped up and seized the canoe. "I am sorry, Fog Man," he said contritely. "Won't you let me go with you? I am really very young and foolish, and I am very lonely."

The stern Fog Man relented and said: "I am going only a short way along the coast. Come with me, if you like."

Sketco jumped in, saying: "I will steer."

Before picking up his paddle, Kanugu put his hat on. Immediately, the mist began to gather along the sea. Kanugu jammed the hat down over his ears, and the fog rolled thicker and thicker.

"Steer straight!" he shouted, plunging the paddle in and swerving the canoe round. "That is not the way I am going."

"I am sorry, Kanugu, but you have made so much fog that I cannot see."

Kanugu grunted and sat brooding under his hat while the fog thickened about the canoe and hid both sea and shore. Because of his sharp eyes, the Raven could see as well as if the sun were shining, but he pretended that the fog blinded him and he kept steering the canoe away from the land, out into the open ocean.

"Where are you steering?" growled the Fog Man.

He dipped his paddle into the water with a powerful sweep as if to turn the canoe, but a strong current seemed to twist it out of his control. Sketco could always handle a paddle with a magic that made up for his puny strength and outplayed the strongest arm.

"I am sorry," he said again, grinning to himself. "The fog bewilders me."

Kanugu took off his straw hat and threw it in the canoe. At once, the fog began to shift and thin out. From a heavy pall, it ravelled into long shreds of mist that let in glimpses of sunshine and sea; then these pale streamers dissolved into wisps of cloud that floated away and disappeared.

The sun was beating on the heaving sea. The shore had vanished: it was not even a smudge on the horizon; and the only land that was to be seen was a small rocky island that lay in front of the rapidly flying canoe.

The Fog Man gasped and looked at the young Raven in amazement.

"Who are you?" he stammered. "Where are you taking us?"

Before Sketco had time to answer, the old man looked at the island and with a cry of dismay clapped the hat on his head. In the blink of Sketco's eyes, the island was swallowed up in fog, and sun and sea were blotted out.

"Why did you shut out the island, Kanugu?" asked Sketco. "I can see through the fog, you know. I am Sketco, the Raven."

The Fog Man did not answer, because he had never heard of Sketco the Raven.

"Your anxiety tells me what I want to know," said Sketco. "That must be the island of the drowned. And that is where I wish to go."

"Oh, no!" the old man cried, trying to deceive him. "That is not the island of the drowned!"

"Where, then, is the island?"

"Eh? What island?" Kanugu stammered, realizing that he had made a mistake.

"The island where the drowned dwell."

"I know of no such place."

Sketco laughed. "Old man, you are not clever enough. Sketco has been seeing the world, yes, both this world and the next, since he left home to seek his uncle and was captured by the Shark People. Take off your hat! I can see through your dismal fog, but it is a nuisance. I like the dry sunshine better."

The Fog Man pressed both hands on top of his head and held his hat down so tightly that the fog seemed to weigh down on Sketco and shoulder him out of the canoe.

"I can't breathe!" he cried and jumping up, he took Kanugu by surprise and wrenched the hat off his head.

The old man shrieked and clutched at it but the Raven held it behind his back and said: "Sit down, Kanugu, or I will tip you into the sea and then you will learn where the island of the drowned lies."

Kanugu sat whimpering in the canoe while the fog cleared away and the island stood, revealed again with the surf beating against its rough, rocky shore.

"Have pity, Raven!" implored the Fog Man. "You cannot go ashore there. No one can go ashore on that island unless he is dead. If you try to take the canoe in, you will drown the both of us."

"I wish to go ashore," said Sketco.

"But you will never escape again, and I — I tell you, the only way we can land is to be drowned."

"I have been in the land of the Ghosts," said the Raven. The canoe was sliding perilously toward the rocks. Kanugu stared at the wild shore in terror. Suddenly he tried to snatch the paddle out of Sketco's hands.

But Sketco shook him off and plunged the paddle into the water. The canoe leapt into the air, describing a swift arc, and landed so suddenly in a grove of spruce trees that Kanugu was jolted out in a shower of green needles. Sketco, scrambling down after him, found the old man lying stunned on the ground.

"Here we are," he said cheerfully, "and not drowned, after all."

The Fog Man groaned. "There are other ways of dying without drowning. All my bones are broken. Oh, oh, oh!"

"Get up, old man!" said Sketco. "You are all whole, except for this." He offered Kanugu the rib which had been given him for a spearhead. Kanugu nearly swooned with fright when he saw the bone. He felt his chest gingerly, groaning the while. The Raven laughed at him. "This is only my harpoon!" he cried.

Not until he had persuaded the Fog Man that what he said was true, would the Fog Man get up. He rose, shaking and moaning, and said: "Where is my hat?"

"I left it in the canoe."

The Raven seized his shoulder.

"Don't touch me!" whined the old man. "I am all bruises."

"Where did you get that canoe?" asked Sketco. "It isn't every canoe that will fly through the air."

"I didn't know the canoe would fly through the air," the old man whimpered.

"It isn't everyone can make it fly through the air. Where did you get that canoe?"

"I made it."

"You lie," said Sketco. "Very well, you shall stay here with the ghosts when I leave the island."

Kanugu burst into tears. "No! no! Do not leave me here!" he pleaded. "I will tell you the truth. I found the canoe drifting on the sea. I swear I did not know it could fly."

"It is my canoe," said Sketco.

"It had a hole in it, and I patched it up."

"The shark made that hole."

"It was all but sunk when I found it," said the Fog Man. "I did not know that anyone owned it, so I towed it home and mended it."

"It is my canoe," repeated the Raven.

"I don't want it. I will gladly give it up, but please take me home. I will go back to my old canoe. I used this because it was so much better, and I am a busy man, with much fog to make."

Sketco stood looking at him, feeling a little vain because the Fog Man, so much older than he was, had proved so cowardly. "Why must you make the fog?" asked Sketco.

The old man looked at him in surprise. "Why?" he repeated.

"Yes. I am learning about the world," said Sketco, "and I should like to know why you make the fog. I can't see much good in it," he added, as Kanugu looked up at him stupidly. "Why do you make it?"

"Why, because I have always made it," said Kanugu.

"Is that the reason?"

"Of course. What other reason could there be?"

"It is for the same reason that the Thunder Man and his daughter ravage the sky with storms," said Sketco. He nodded wisely. "I am learning about the world."

"Why did you come here? This is not the world."

"I came to find my drowned brothers and to take them away with me."

Kanugu shuddered. "I will sit here under the trees and wait for you," he said.

"Do not run away with the canoe!" said Sketco. He laughed and disappeared into the woods.

"Where are you, my brothers?" the Raven called, as he tramped over the island. It was a small rocky island with no sign of life except for a few twisted junipers and the spruce trees. No bird fluttered and there was no sound save the beating of the surf. Sketco sat down upon a rock despondently, with his chin in his hand, listening, however, with both ears.

A scream startled him and he bounded quickly over the springy juniper to where he had left Kanugu.

"The tide!" cried the old man hoarsely. "The tide is rising! The island will claim us, after all! We shall be drowned!"

Slowly, and then more quickly, and quicker yet, the tide rose. Sketco and the Fog Man swarmed up the trees and climbed into the canoe, which still rested in the branches. But the sea followed them. For a moment, the canoe floated, and then, with a swirl, the water drew it down, choking off the Fog Man's bleat. To the very tree-tops, the island was swallowed by the sea.

Sketco and Kanugu found themselves floating under the water. With a deft stroke of the paddle, the Raven loosened the canoe from the trees and sent it shooting outward. He thought it would dart to the top, but it remained suspended in the water like a fish, yielding gracefully to his paddle, driving ahead, circling, dipping its prow and sinking, rising, but never escaping to the upper air.

"This is like being in the country of the Shark People!" exclaimed Sketco. "How cool it is! How green and quiet!"

"It is the country of the drowned," groaned Kanugu. "We are both dead!"

"Here, put on your hat!"

But the Fog Man was in no mood for joking.

All around them, the water shimmered, pale green as the light filtered through. Weeds waving very slowly reached out with languorous fingers to touch the canoe, and fish like shadows drifted by.

"It is not very deep here," said Sketco.

"It is deep enough," Kanugu sighed.

"Look!" the Raven whispered. "Is that a shark, or what is it? — It looks like another canoe."

Kanugu started. "It is our shadow," he said in a moment. Then he added, "But how can it be our shadow? We are nothing but shadows ourselves."

It was a long canoe with seven men in it, paddling swiftly and silently. They raised their paddles in salute and glided out of sight.

"We are their new neighbours," said Kanugu dolefully. "Who will make the fog now?"

"Your hat is here," Sketco said curtly. "Fog is drowned, too. The world will be better without it."

Kanugu shook his head and sighed.

The canoe floated on, passing several others in the distance, until it beached on a point that jutted out into the sea. It was the lip of an island that seemed to float midway in the green water and yet remain steady.

"Have we come back to the same island?" asked Sketco. "Have we been travelling in circles?" But Kanugu did not answer. He had put on his hat and it failed to add to the dimness of the drowned world.

The two stepped out of the canoe and walked up the beach until they came to a village which lay between the woods and the sand.

"This must be the other side of the island," Sketco thought. Children were playing about the houses and men were busy mending nets and patching canoes and sharpening spearheads, while the women were weaving baskets and tending fires that had neither flames nor smoke. The village was submerged in the green water and the people moved about in it as if it were only dim light. Silently they greeted the newcomers and Sketco discovered that although they understood the movement of his lips they did not hear his voice.

"I am Sketco, the Raven," he said. "I have come to find my brothers who were drowned by their uncle."

Three small boys, who were tossing quoits, looked up at him, dropped their game and quietly came to his side. They could not speak, but the Raven knew that he had found his brothers.

"Jump into the canoe," he said. "I am going to take you home."

Meekly, the boys did as they were told, while the villagers looked on, impassive.

Kanugu climbed in wearily, sank down into the bottom of the canoe and immediately fell asleep.

Sketco smiled at him and, glancing at the little boys, who sat close together, clasping each other's hands, he shoved off and jumped into the canoe himself. But no sooner had he lifted the paddle than it fell from his hands and he too sank down in slumber.

When Sketco awoke, he found that the canoe was floating just at the edge of the island. The Fog Man was still huddled up, asleep, but the three brothers had vanished. The island was above the sea and the sun was pouring its light on it. Sketco rubbed his eyes. It was the same beach, but he could not see the village. There were no canoes on the water but his own; there were no houses; no men mending nets, no women weaving baskets, no children playing; it was the same beach, but it was high and dry above the water, and it was empty, and Sketco's brothers were not to be seen.

The Raven cried in his disappointment and then prodded the Fog Man with his paddle.

"Eh!" grunted Kanugu, starting up and blinking at the sun. He sat up abruptly. He jumped up. He shouted and pinched himself. He put his hat on. As he saw the fog begin to gather over the sand and rise into the trees, his astonishment gave way to delight.

"Then we are alive!" he cried.

"Wretch!" growled Sketco, pulling the hat off and sending it spinning out into the ocean. "You have no thought for anyone but yourself and your fog."

As Kanugu swam after his hat, Sketco crouched down in the canoe and buried his head in his hands.

At last he rose, dipped the paddle into the sea and with a stroke left the island far behind him.

The fog began to gather again because Kanugu, swimming frantically after the canoe, had been obliged to put his hat on so that he could have his hands free.

When he saw this, the Raven waited. He said nothing while Kanugu climbed into the canoe and took the hat off.

"Let us get away from here," the old man gasped. "The island is swallowed by the tide every evening. We may be trapped again."

Sketco did not hear him. He was dreaming. Suddenly he lifted his paddle high in the air, with a look of joy on his face. He brought the paddle down with a splash and as he did so cried "Kuk!"

At that moment, the three little shadows, who had been sitting unseen in the canoe all the time, came to life. When Kanugu saw the boys appear, he gasped with amazement. But Sketco slapped their small bodies and rejoiced when he felt their flesh and heard the sound of his hand upon it.

"You have come back to life!" he shouted, as he brought his paddle down and sent the canoe streaking across the sea.

CHAPTER 8

THE SHADOW BOYS

"Where are you going now?" asked Kanugu timidly, as the canoe shot over the waves, scooting like a duck and scarcely touching the water.

"To the far North, to my father's village," Sketco answered. The old man sat clutching the sides of the canoe with both hands, and his face was warped with misery.

"I am old," he said, "and I shall die soon enough. I cannot go so far, at such a speed. And I have my work to do: the fog must be made or the world will go wrong."

"What shall we do with him, brothers?" the Raven asked mischievously.

The boys did not answer.

"Shall I dump him in the sea?"

"No more! No more! I cannot swim as well as I could when I was young! I will sink and be drowned! Take me," the Fog Man prayed, "to the mainland and set me down anywhere. I can walk home."

"What do you think, brothers?"

But the boys did not even smile. Sketco looked at their glum little faces. "Are you frightened?" he asked gently. "Never mind, we shall soon be home. Then you will see your mother and father again!"

He paddled the canoe swiftly to shore and waited for Kanugu to climb out.

"Thank you, thank you!" said the old man fervently. "If you ever need any fog in a hurry, call upon me." He hobbled along the beach with his hat under his arm. The Raven shouted as the canoe swerved and leapt into the sea like something alive, and in a twinkling, Kanugu, who had turned his head to see it go, saw nothing but the rolling waves.

"Well, brothers," said the Raven, "you have not grown in all the years you have lived below with the shadows."

"Ghosts do not grow," said one of the little fellows.

"Never mind. You are alive again. You have bodies, and now you will grow up to be strong men and mighty hunters."

The boys did not answer. They sat close together and Sketco was surprised to see how sober they were.

"Why, what ails you?" he asked. "Surely you are eager to grow up to be hunters? to spear the salmon and harpoon the whales? and kill the bears? and go to war, like other men?"

The boys sat silent.

"Have you no wish for strong arms and supple wrists and keen eyes? Would you not like to paddle a canoe and roam over the world looking for new things?"

Sketco's brothers looked sad and wistfully shook their heads.

The Raven in amazement stopped his paddle in mid-air and stared at them. He dropped the paddle into the canoe and seized first one boy and then another.

"You are flesh!" he cried. "There are bones in your shoulders! There is blood under your skin!" He gazed at them with grief in his eyes. "Will you not hunt your cruel uncle and avenge your death? Ah!" he sighed, "you have been dead too long."

"It is too late, Sketco," said one of the brothers.

"We are older than you," said the second, "and yet we are younger. We do not wish to grow up."

"I am taking you to your mother, who has wailed many nights for you," said the Raven. "Will you not go to her?"

"We will go," said the brothers, "but we do not belong to this world. We cannot stay."

"We live under the sea."

"Where the sun does not shine so fiercely."

The little boys sat close together with their heads down and their eyes shut tightly.

"Come!" exclaimed the Raven. "You have lived too long in the dark. You are not yet used to the sun. You are small and a little afraid, but we will soon make men of you!"

The brothers sat dejected and did not open their mouths.

"Do you remember your home?" Sketco asked them.

They nodded. "I was very lonely, at first," one of them replied, "and afraid. When my brothers came, I was happy."

He winced. "This sun burns me!" he complained. "And yet I am cold!"

"My knees hurt," said another, "and my eyes ache."

The third crouched in misery and did not speak.

"We are home!" shouted Sketco as the canoe slid on the beach. "Come, brothers! Run! Surprise your mother! Wake up! Hurry!"

The boys were reluctant to get out of the canoe, so

Sketco smacked them with good-natured gusto. The tingling of their skin made them cry, but they scurried across the sand.

They walked very gingerly up the little trail, complaining that their feet hurt.

When the villagers saw Sketco and his three brothers appear out of the sea, they were astonished, because they did not know who it could be, but Sketco hailed them with lusty shouts: "Do you not know us, then? I am Sketco, the Raven, and these are my three brothers who were drowned!" As he spoke, Sketco thrust out his chest and put his head to one side arrogantly.

Half afraid, the villagers drew back. "Sketco!" they murmured. "How tall he has grown! I remember the children who were drowned. They went fishing with their uncle. And they never came back. How the mother grieved for them! And Sketco went out to seek them. He has brought them back from the dead! They look frightened. Are they really alive? Or are they ghosts?" The villagers shrank away.

"You need not be afraid of small boys!" laughed Sketco. "But I must tell you," he added proudly, "I have great medicine. I have lived with the sharks, and I have fished for whale with the Thunder Man! I have fooled Kanugu, the Fog Man, and I have brought my brothers back from the island of the drowned. And I have here a harpoon head which I stole from the Ghosts in the land of shadows! This is only the beginning of my wonders!"

While he was lying and boasting, the three bewildered little brothers crouched down on the ground, close together, and wept.

"Come, my little brothers," said Sketco tenderly, as he leaned over them and gently touched their shoulders. "You need not be afraid."

The news of their coming spread quickly and before they had gone many steps the mother came running down to where the crowd was gathered. "My sons! My sons!" she cried, gathering the little boys in her arms and weeping. She squeezed them until they cried and then she turned and drew the Raven to her. "Is this my brave son, Sketco? How big he is! My youngest, and yet my eldest! You have filled my heart with joy!" She wept.

The Raven looked at her with sadness in his eyes, for he remembered what his brothers had said, and he could see that they were not happy. The mother soon saw this for herself.

"Our sons are strange," she said to the father. "They are not happy. They do not laugh and play like other boys, as they used to, before their uncle took them out to fish. They sit and dream and never say a word, and they do not seem to know how to eat. They are falling thin, and they are always cold."

"They are too tender," said the father.

The mother became anxious over them and tried to coax them to laugh, but they only smiled sadly.

"What troubles you?" she asked at last. "Are you not glad to be back with us again? My heart has ached for you these many years. Can you not be happy?"

The boys sat staring out to sea, or they crouched by the fire and watched the smoke curl up and drift out through the smoke-hole to the sky. They cared for nothing else.

"We do not belong to this world," said one, wretchedly.

"We live with the drowned, under the sea," said the second.

The third little son looked mutely at her.

The mother went away weeping. She appealed to Sketco, but Sketco only shrugged his shoulders.

"It seems," he said, "as if the dead may not come back."

The following morning the brothers came to Sketco and stood silently in front of him.

The Raven looked down at them sadly. "I know what you would say, my brothers. You must have your way."

They followed him out of the house. He turned sharply. "Take leave of your mother!" he cried. "Have you no love in your hearts?"

Their faces were sad but impassive as their mother, in anguish, bade them farewell and their father stood watching sullenly.

They neither smiled nor uttered a word when Sketco shoved the canoe out into the sea and stood up to salute the puzzled neighbours of the village. They sat in the canoe and looked straight ahead.

Swift as a bird, the canoe darted over the water and the land quickly fled from sight. Islands and wheeling gulls disappeared, and at last there was nothing to see but the great gloomy ocean on every hand and the vast sullen sky over-head, nothing but the sky and the sea and on the horizon in front a small cloud of fog.

Sketco sat brooding with his paddle resting, his eyes scarcely aware of the little cloud that was growing and growing and filling both sea and sky with thick grey mist. He came to with a start at the sound of a splash.

He was alone in the canoe.

"My brothers!" he cried. But there was no answer.

Where the little boys had sat, there was nothing but fog.

Sadly the Raven turned the canoe and slowly he paddled back toward the shore.

Looming up in the gloom, he saw the blurred outline of a man in a canoe. The man wore a wide straw hat pulled down over his face.

"Kanugu," said Sketco softly to himself. "It is better that the Fog Man should keep his secrets."

He went home to console his mother and father, but he did not stay long with them.

"I must go out again," he said. "When I first went, it was with two missions, to restore my brothers to you from the dead and to avenge their death. The first I have accomplished." He shrugged his shoulders. "It is always too late to bring back the dead," he said sadly. "But the other thing I can do. My uncle murdered my brothers. Because of him, you are heartbroken; because of him, they may never more enjoy life, they may never grow up to be strong lusty men. There is nothing I can do that will be punishment enough for this crime. For he has lived his life, and death will come to him as a welcome sleep. There would be no one who would wish him back. But death may be a long time coming to him, and it is not right that he should go about the world working evil."

"Goodbye, Sketco," said his mother. "You have a good heart. Will you take something with you to stay you on your long journey?"

"No," said Sketco proudly. "I am no longer a child. I have the ghost bone which I will sharpen into a harpoon, and I have my wits and the power of my magic. I am Sketco, the Raven, and I have mighty things to do in the world."

CHAPTER 9

HOW THE RAVEN BROUGHT THE FIRE

Many moons waxed and waned on the Raven's wanderings. Sometimes he used his wings as the Raven and sometimes he paddled his canoe as a young Indian growing into a youth supple and strong and tall; sometimes he left his canoe hidden under branches and leaves on the shore and tramped through the woods, up the hills and through the mountain passes and down to the level plains.

It was while he was travelling and searching that he discovered the race of Man grovelling in the darkness and took pity on its wretchedness. By trickery he cheated the miser, Nass-shig-ee-yalth out of his hoard, burst the bag of stars over the sky and sent the sun and moon rolling round the earth.

"In my world," said the Raven to himself, "the light is shared by all. Why should it not be so in the world of Man?" He was well pleased when he saw how the Indians benefited from the sun but later, as he walked about among the people or stood with arms folded watching them, he knitted his brows in a frown. Something was lacking. The sun gave light and warmth. But the nights were cold, even when the moon shed its lustre over the villages; some days the sun was shut out by fog and rain; and in winter it came late and departed early. The Indians lived on roots and berries and raw flesh and fish.

Suddenly the Raven realized what was missing. Fire! "Who is hoarding the fire that belongs to mankind?" he asked.

No one could answer him, for no one knew even what fire was. So Sketco ranged the world looking for a sign of smoke.

He found it in the far North, as he was hovering over the solitary island where Qok, the great Snowy Owl, lives. Smoke, a faint wisp, was rising up from the hole in Qok's roof. "Ah," said the Raven, "Qok has the fire! I will persuade him to give me some."

Sketco swooped to the ground and, at the sound of his wings, the Snowy Owl came stumbling out.

"Who is it?" he asked querulously, blinking as if he had been wakened from a sound sleep.

"It is Sketco, the Raven."

"What do you want?" the great owl asked, ruffling his white feathers impatiently. "I came to the North to be quiet. Why do you break in upon my sleep?"

"Qok," said the Raven politely," you have the fire . . ."

Snowy Owl raised his wings menacingly and Sketco, who was much smaller, started back in alarm. "Go away!" Qok screamed. "Do you think I could keep warm up here in this cold country if I did not have a little fire? Go away, I tell you! Leave me in peace!"

The Raven, keeping a respectful distance, murmured: "You have a good coat of heavy feathers . . ." He raised his voice as the owl turned his back and went into the house. "Qok, will you not share your fire with the people? I have given them the light of the moon and the stars for their comfort and their pleasure, and the warmth of the sun, but it is not enough. Winter comes and even the sun cannot keep away the cold. Will you give . . . ?"

But Qok turned suddenly, rolling his goggle eyes and flapping his enormous white wings, and drove Sketco into the sea.

"Very well, Snowy Owl," said the Raven to himself, as he rose in the air and steered south, "if you will not give, I will take."

After days of scheming, he called the Ermine to him.

"My friend," he said to the little animal, "you are small and you are nimble. From what I have heard, you are clever, too." The Ermine squirmed and smiled. "Will you do me a service?"

"Gladly," said the Ermine.

"Listen carefully," the Raven went on. "You have your fur and you can keep warm in the coldest night. But the poor Indians are naked. They need fire . . ."

The Ermine blinked questioningly.

"Do you know Qok, the Snowy Owl?"

The Ermine nodded.

"He keeps the fire to himself," said the Raven. "Hidden away in his house. Will you go to him and steal some of his fire?"

The little Ermine's eyes sparkled and he flicked his tail. "With pleasure!" he exclaimed. "I will leave him cold!"

"You need not take *all* his heat away," said Sketco, with a smile. "Be careful that he doesn't snap you up in that sharp beak of his."

"He might as well try to catch the wind!" boasted the Ermine. He slipped away.

He lost no time in reaching the island and deftly he wriggled his way into the Snowy Owl's house. Qok was dozing by the fire. The Ermine grinned. "This will be easy," he thought, as he scampered across the floor without a sound. In a twinkling, he snatched a burning coal from the fire. He popped it into his mouth. He could not help uttering a little exclamation of pain as it stung his tongue and brought the tears to his eyes. It was the smallest of sounds, but the Snowy Owl opened his great eyes and caught sight of him.

"Who are you? What are you doing in my house?" he demanded, rising and spreading out his wings.

The Ermine gulped and dared not answer.

Qok started toward him. "Speak!" he cried angrily. "Answer me! Are you dumb?"

The poor little Ermine could only shrink and tremble in terror, so the owl struck him on the head with one of his broad wings. The coal dropped out of the Ermine's mouth, and he flew out of the house squealing in terror.

"I must try another way," said the Raven, when he heard the Ermine's shamefaced report. He puzzled and pondered a long time and at last he decided to go again himself.

This time, instead of appearing as the Raven or in his human form, he disguised himself as a deer. In those days, the Deer had a long tail, like the Wolf, and when the Raven put on his deerskin he dipped the long bushy tail in pitch.

Before going north to the home of the Snowy Owl, he called a jay to him. "Jay," he said, "I am Sketco, the Raven. Will you carry a message for me to Qok?"

The Jay agreed to go. "What do you wish me to say?"

"Tell him a handsome young chief is coming to dance for him and his people."

"Shall I say it is the Raven?"

"No! No! Do not mention the Raven."

"Is he not a handsome young chief?" asked the Jay, with a supercilious smile.

"That may be, but it is the Deer who will dance."

When he flew north, Jay found the Owl spluttering in his usual bad temper. "Why do you come here to bother me?" he snapped. "Am I never to be left at peace in my own house?"

"A handsome young chief is coming to dance for you and your people," Jay quoted faithfully.

"Dance!" screamed Qok. "Dance! I'll have no dancing here! Now get out or I'll make *you* dance!"

Jay retreated politely, bowing and scraping his wings.

"This great chief," he said in a flattering tone, "has heard of your magnificence and he is coming many miles to honour you."

The Snowy Owl lowered his wings and stood blinking his goggle eyes. "He is a great chief?" he asked in a harsh voice.

"Oh, one of the first of chiefs!"

"You say he knows of me?"

"Is there anyone who doesn't know you? Although you do live such a retired, quiet life."

The great Snowy Owl began to puff out his white feathers and preen himself. "I will give a sumptuous feast," said he.

"Would you like me to send out the invitations?" asked the Jay ingratiatingly.

"Eh? Yes, that would be a good idea," the Owl agreed pompously. "Yes, we must have invitations. Of course, invitations, by all means."

He did not like to admit that he did not know whom to ask, for he lived such a churlish life that he had no friends.

So the Jay busied himself inviting the guests while the Snowy Owl went fussing about the house, preening his feathers, piling more fuel on the fire, and squinting his eyes to see if the handsome young chief was coming.

The Raven stepped into his canoe and sat in the middle, dressed in his deerskin blanket with the long tail. For escort, he had a flock of seagulls and a flock of crows.

Swiftly they flew over the ocean and when they reached the island in the North, Qok came fluttering and stumbling down to the shore to welcome them and conduct them to his house. The Jay had been tireless and a host of birds and animals was gathered about the splendid fire, as much out of curiosity to see the surly Owl as to see the dance.

"You shall be greatly honoured, Noble Chief," said Qok. who had no suspicion that the dancing deer was really the crafty Raven come to filch his fire. "You shall be greatly honoured," he stammered, "as — as you have — as you are honouring me in coming to my poor house." He spluttered and coughed and glared at a young rabbit as if he would have eaten him. Indeed, had he not been on his best behaviour, nothing would have pleased him better than to have devoured the tender young rabbit, who had been foolish to come so near the house. But he had to remember the grace of hospitality.

Surrounded by the gulls and crows, the Deer marched into the house and was received with great clamour. When he came to dance, the birds and animals cleared the floor for him and began to beat time by clapping their paws and wings and striking the floor with their tails and stamping their feet. Some pounded on drums, some made a steady clatter with sticks, and they all began to sing at the top of their voices.

Slowly, the Deer circled the room, wagging his head, holding his tail stiff, and planting his feet firmly on the ground, one in front of the other. Then suddenly he began to run and skip and jump, faster and faster. The animals shouted with glee and the birds shrieked and whistled, beating time, quicker, quicker, quicker. The great Snowy Owl sat with his wings folded, blinking his eyes and nodding benevolently.

He was bewildered and his head swam, he did not understand it at all, but he was flattered (although no one paid any attention to him) and he said: "He is a beautiful dancer, the noble young chief. We are honoured to have him here, and he shall be richly rewarded."

No one heeded him in the noise, but the Raven heard him. "You do not know how richly I shall be rewarded, Snowy Owl!" he exclaimed to himself, as he pranced about in the deerskin.

He whirled and sprang forward and jumped back and did everything but turn somersaults, while the guests whistled and shouted with delight and the Snowy Owl sat nodding and smiling foolishly.

The Deer edged closer and closer to the fire, but no one dreamed what was in his mind. Suddenly he backed into the fire and thrust his long tail into the flames. Because it had been rubbed with pitch, it caught quickly and was soon ablaze.

With his tail flaring behind him, the Deer made a dash for the door and before anyone had recovered enough from his astonishment to move, he was flying down to the sea.

At first the birds and animals thought it was an accident, and when their surprise let them free, they wanted to rush out and help him. Qok's house was full of beating wings and tumbling fur as everyone tried to push out of the door at the same time.

The Snowy Owl was dumbfounded, but he quickly came to his senses and screamed: "He is stealing my fire! Stop him! Catch him! He is stealing my fire!"

He struggled to get out, but by the time he managed to shoulder through the clamouring crowd, it was only to see the Raven's canoe disappearing southward.

"Chase him!" shrieked Qok hoarsely. "The villain! The wretch! The ingrate! He has stolen my fire!"

But it was too late. Even the eagles could not overtake the Raven. At last nothing could be seen but the flaming tail, twinkling like a star, and soon that, too, disappeared from sight.

The seagulls and the crows laughed so merrily that all the other birds set on them and drove them helter-skelter across the ocean, threatening to peck their eyes out.

The Snowy Owl huddled in a corner of his house, sobbing from grief and rage. "Never," he said bitterly, "never again will I give a dance. I did not know there was so much deceit in the world."

As soon as the Raven reached the country of the Indians, he jumped out of the canoe and began tearing through the woods. When the people saw the deer with the blazing tail, they shouted with alarm and began to run away. As he passed, his flaming tail brushed through the trees, striking here a spruce, there a cedar, somewhere else a maple, until a tree of every kind that grows was alight and flaring in the woods. At last, when his tail was burned to a stump, the Deer pounded it out on a stone and sank down exhausted.

The fires in the woods began to spread and the Indians, instead of being thankful for their blessing, fled for their lives. But the Raven threw off his deerskin and appeared before them and showed them how to put out the flames with water.

"Now, my friends," he said, "I have brought you fire, to cook your food and keep you warm. Be careful of it and it will serve you well. Be master of it or it will master you."

"You brought it," said one man, pointing to the charred, smoking trees, "but you killed it again."

"No," said the Raven. "It is still in the wood. It sleeps. Let me teach you how to wake it up again." And he showed them how to make fire-drills and how to kindle a flame.

"It is in the stones, too," he explained. "I put it in both wood and stone so that you should always have it." He showed them how to strike sparks out of the flint before he left them. "Teach these things to your children," he said, "and your people need never be cold, even when it is winter, or when it is night, or when the world is drenched with rain."

"But the water kills the fire," protested the man who had spoken before.

"Can you not keep wood ready in a dry place?" Sketco asked. "And you must teach your children, too, that water stamps out fire. For sometimes fire must be killed."

From that day to this, there has been fire in the world for the use of Man. But the island where Qok, the Snowy Owl, lives has gone cold, and now they say that it is the great Snowy Owl, sailing out of the North and ruffling his feathers to keep himself warm, who brings the soft white snow.

CHAPTER 10

THE MAN WHO SAT ON THE TIDE

Not satisfied with bringing the Indians light and fire, the Raven set about teaching them better ways of living. He taught them how to cut down trees and build houses; to hollow out the tall cedars into canoes; to steam wood and bend it, even to stitch it with spruce root fibres; to shape it into dishes and make it into boxes. He taught them how to weave mats and baskets and straw hats out of red cedar bark and the roots of spruce trees; how to spin nettles into fishing-nets; how to make blankets out of mountain goat wool. Once they had crawled in the dark and huddled in holes in the ground, gnawing bitter roots and munching green berries; now they walked abroad in the sunlight, built themselves houses, plunged into the sea in canoes, hunted and fished, lived lustily, fought among themselves and strove for power, and carved lofty totem poles as monuments to their pride. But they owed all their life to the

Raven, going about among them from tribe to tribe, so lost in his teaching and his building that he did not take count of the flying years. It was Sketco who taught them how to polish stone hammers and sharpen bone knives, how to harpoon whales, porpoises and seals, how to make hemlock hooks for the catching of halibut and cod; it was he who scattered the salmon eggs in the rivers and showed the Indians how to catch salmon in traps and weirs. He taught them how to squeeze oil out of the oolachen and how to cook food with hot stones in the wooden boxes. They were not always grateful to the Raven, but they prospered.

In the course of time, however, some of the tribes proved to be less fortunate than others; they were unlucky in fishing and they fell powerless before the stronger men who raided their villages, robbed them and sometimes carried them off into slavery.

Their chiefs came complaining to the Raven. "We are starving," they told him.

"If we could only reach the food that lies at the bottom of the ocean we should have enough to eat, but the water is very deep. Some of our young men have dived down, but they have never come back."

"I will do what I can to help you," promised the Raven.

He pushed off in his canoe and peered down through the sea. "There is an abundance of food at the bottom of the ocean," he said to himself. "I must find some way of getting it for these unfortunate people." For a long time he sat with his chin in his hand, gazing at the water and thinking. "If I dive down and bring some back, it will not be enough to go round, and I cannot plunge down into the sea every day, unless I turn into a fish, and I would rather be a bird or a man." He remembered the Shark People in their dim underwater world.

He drifted along, puzzling his brain. "I have magic," he thought sadly, "but I cannot teach the strong tribes to leave these poor people at peace. I can teach men how to make hooks and nets and how to catch fish but I cannot give them brains to learn the art of living together."

He wondered if he could shove the ocean aside so that the unfortunates could swarm over the bottom and rake up the shellfish and the sea-plants, but he did not know how to do it.

"Ah!" the thought suddenly struck him. "The Fog Man! Perhaps old Kanugu can tell me." He dipped his paddle with a brisk turn of the wrist and struck off northward.

Soon he saw Kanugu, squatting in his canoe, with his

nose tilted, sniffing the air. Just as Sketco drew alongside, the old man picked up his straw hat and was about to put it carefully upon his head.

"Wait, Kanugu!" shouted the Raven, laying his hand on the old man's arm. "Have you no manners? Would you throw a fog in the face of a friend who has come to visit you?"

The Fog Man dropped his hat in the canoe and looked suspiciously at Sketco.

"I am not going to the island!" he said hurriedly.

"Your memory is good, old man!" said Sketco. "But I have something else to do, this time. You know the secrets of the sea . . ."

The old man grunted and shifted uneasily in his canoe. "Can you tell me," asked Sketco, "how to push the ocean to one side?"

"Why do you bother me with such foolish questions? I have work to do."

Kanugu reached for his hat.

"There is more important work to do than making fog," said the Raven, restraining the old man's hand.

"Not for me," said Kanugu in a surly growl. "I am the Fog Man."

"You must admit that fog-making is not very constructive! Now my work is to help mankind, to build, to teach, to feed . . ."

"My work is making fog," Kanugu said curtly.

"I am sorry if I have offended you, Fog Man. All I ask is that you help me. I want to get food for the people who are starving."

The old man snorted. "By moving the sea?"

"Yes. There is food at the bottom that they cannot reach."

"Why do you bother me? I have nothing to do with the bottom of the sea. My work is on top." He sniffed the air again. "It is time I put on my hat . . . You had better speak to the Man Who Sits on the Tide," he added, without looking at the Raven.

"Ah! Where is he?"

The Fog Man pointed northward, along the shoreline.

"That rock?"

Kanugu shrugged his shoulders.

Sketco strained his eyes and peered more closely at the figure in the distance. "Is it a man sitting in the water?"

The Fog Man reached for his hat and did not answer.

Sketco laughed. "I will go and ask him. Why does he sit there so still?"

"He has his work to do, and I have mine," Kanugu answered shortly. He jammed the hat down on his head.

But before the fog had time to gather, Sketco snatched it off, tossed it into his own canoe, and paddled off, laughing merrily.

With a cry of consternation and rage, the Fog Man paddled after him, but Sketco's canoe slid so swiftly over the water that Kanugu was left far behind.

"The people shall have a clear day," said the Raven to himself. "I brought them the sun and I am tired of Kanugu's blotting it out."

He steered for what appeared to be a solitary crag jutting up from the shore. It was really the Man Who Sits on the Tide. The old giant, who crouched in the water close to shore, with his knees drawn up to his chin, embracing his legs with his clasped hands, looked up but did not blink as Sketco's canoe scooted past his shins. But a flock of seagulls that had settled on his shoulders and built nests in his hair hurled itself into the sky, screaming and beating white wings in the sun.

"Hi, old man!" shouted the Raven, prodding the giant with his paddle.

The Man Who Sits on the Tide did not answer, so the Raven struck him smartly on the shin.

At that, the giant howled and kicked out with such force that he made a great wave, which swamped Kanugu's canoe half a mile away and pitched the Fog Man into the sea. As for Sketco, he deftly turned his canoe as he hit the old man and dodged behind his back. Moaning, the giant rubbed his leg with both hands, but he did not get up out of the water.

"I am sorry if I hurt you," said the Raven, appearing again, "but you seem to be deaf, and I like to have answers to my questions. I am Sketco, the Raven, and I ask a good many."

The old man looked at him mournfully and shook a young seagull out of his ear with a toss of his head.

"Why do you not get up?"

"I am sitting on the tide."

"Why are you sitting on the tide?"

The giant frowned and, still rubbing his leg with one hand, asked: "Why did you strike me?"

"To attract your attention. You did not hear me call. You seem to be engulfed in thought. What are you thinking of?"

"Sitting on the tide."

"Do you think of nothing else?"

The old man frowned again. "No. It is my life work."

"Why do you sit on the tide?"

"Because I have always sat on the tide."

"Oh, that is no answer!" cried the Raven angrily. "I am always hearing that answer and it means nothing! Get up! Get up! *Get up!*" He jabbed the giant in the knee with his harpoon. The old fellow roared with pain and jumped up, hugging his wound with both hands. Sketco dodged behind him and jabbed him in the buttocks. With a yell, the old man turned and tried to clutch his tormentor. But the Raven was too quick for him and kept out of his reach.

A strange thing happened while the giant stamped and plunged about. There was a loud noise, like an enormous gurgling and sucking, and the sea began to sink. It was pouring like a torrent into a huge hole in the bottom. The current was so strong that Sketco had the greatest difficulty in keeping his canoe from being gulped down. With a skilful stroke, he beached it.

When the giant saw that the earth was drinking the sea, he ran frantically to staunch the flow by sitting down on the hole again, but Sketco prodded him with the sharp harpoon and chased him ashore jumping and yelping and crying for help.

"So that is your secret!" said the Raven, pricking him again.

"Let me sit down!" wailed the old man.

"I should think you would be too sore to sit down for a while! You should take a little exercise," said the Raven. "You have been squatting there in the sea too long. Jump! Dance!"

Greedily the earth drank the ocean, with great gurgling and slobbering, and the old man, jumping up and down, moaned: "The sea will dry up! The sea will dry up!"

He made a sudden dash at Sketco, as if to bowl him over with a blow of his mighty hand, but the Raven caught him in the ribs with his harpoon and the giant tumbled over backward and lay gasping on the wet sand.

For miles along the shore, the ocean had sunk, leaving the sand and sludge underneath exposed for the first time since sea and sand were made. Sketco was too busy watching the old man to notice, but Kanugu was plodding along wearily, the earth pulling at his feet at every step, doggedly pushing toward Sketco, intent on getting back his fog hat.

The poor Indians in the villages, when they saw the sea sinking and shrinking away from the shore, ran down with joyous shouts and were soon dragging home an abundant harvest. "The Raven has kept his promise!" they cried, as they tore up the tresses of seaweed and pried mussels and clams off the rocks which had been submerged by the sea.

Sketco kept the Man Who Sits on the Tide hopping about and groaning for hours, until he was satisfied that the people had gathered enough to feast them many a day and night, and then he said: "Old man, you may sit down again on your hole and stop the sea from ebbing away entirely. We need the sea, we cannot get along without it altogether, but it must budge a little now and again and yield to the land. Hereafter, you must get up twice a day, in the morning and in the evening."

The Man Who Sits on the Tide rose stiffly from the sand. "Do you hear?" asked the Raven, pretending to run him through with his spear. The giant cringed and threw up his hands to defend himself. "Answer!" cried the Raven.

"I hear," the giant said hoarsely. Then suddenly, as if he realized that he was bigger than Sketco and older, he spluttered: "Who are you, coming here and pricking me and upsetting my life? I have been sitting on the tide since creation."

"I like to upset things. I am Sketco, the Raven. The world was dark. I upset light into it." He smiled. "And I upset Nass-shig-ee-yalth, too! Just as he hoarded the light, Qok hoarded the fire, but the world was cold, so I upset Qok. And now I have upset you! And I shall go on upsetting, for upsetting is my work in the world."

"I will go back and sit on the tide and I will not move again," said the giant, glowering at him.

The Raven laughed. "We shall see!" he cried. "In the meantime, your precious ocean is running away."

The Man Who Sits on the Tide turned as if he had been struck and limped as quickly as he could toward his hole, keeping a wary eye on the Raven, jumping back with a squeal and a splash when Sketco in fun lunged at him with his spear.

Gingerly, he bent his limbs and sat down on the gushing water, but because he was sore he did not sit down solidly at first and, although the flood was quenched, the sea trickled away slowly under his flanks. He settled himself gradually, frowning balefully at Sketco and grinding his teeth.

"You need not be ugly," the Raven said. "You must become flexible and learn new habits."

The flow at last ceased and the sea began to fill up again, brimming and running out to the shore as high as ever.

Kanugu, lifted by the tide, swam to shore and seized his hat, which was lying in Sketco's canoe. The Raven saw him and laughed.

"You had a weary trudge, old Fog Man!" he said. "I think I upset you, too! But I have found out how to push the sea back and nothing else matters."

Glaring at him wrathfully, Kanugu put his hat on, folded his arms and sat on the sand sulking all night and all next day. There never was a heavier fog.

The Man Who Sits on the Tide fixed himself firmly on his old seat and was determined that nothing should budge him. But the Raven reminded him with the sharp prong of his harpoon, and he soon moved without being told. At first, he was stubborn and he lashed out viciously, but Sketco gave him no rest.

Years afterwards, when someone asked him why he rose up and sat down in the sea, making the tides so regularly, he scratched his head and replied: "Because I have always done so."

CHAPTER 11

THE GAME MOTHER

"Am I growing old?" the Raven asked himself, as he flew on his broad, black wings high above the treetops. "My brain seems dull. I have lost my cunning. I, who taught the people how to get food, myself go hungry." His keen eye caught a glimpse of the Man Who Sits on the Tide, with the water lapping round his thighs and the gulls circling his head in the sunlight. The Raven suddenly chuckled to himself. "I, the great upsetter, myself upset!"

Turning his back on the sea, he wandered far inland, sometimes flying, sometimes walking, exploring the world beyond the mountains and trying to make his living as a hunter. Sometimes he stood in a swift-running river and speared a salmon with his harpoon; with the haft, sometimes he struck a porcupine; sometimes he felled a rabbit, but he fared meagerly and he was far from satisfied. He was glad when he came, one evening, upon the campfire of a party of hunters.

"Where is all the game?" he asked boldly. "I have seen no caribou, no deer, no bears, and I have been hunting many weeks."

"We have had no better luck than you, stranger," said one of the hunters. "Our villages are starving, and we can bring them nothing but a few puny porcupines."

"And owls," another man put in, sourly. "They are dull-witted birds in the daylight and they let themselves be knocked down."

"We cannot live on owls and porcupines," complained the hunters.

"Where are the caribou? the deer? the bears?"

The men shrugged their shoulders. "At the best of times, they are swift, too swift for our arrows."

"We might as well try to shoot the wind."

"We might as well try to snare the sunlight on the water."

"Sometimes we catch them by lucky chance, but now I think Atsentma, the Game Mother, has called them all home."

"Atsentma?" The Raven frowned.

"Yes. She lives in the far North. The game belongs to her and does her bidding."

"She has no love for mankind."

The Raven sat frowning. "I think I have work to do," he muttered to himself.

"May I spend the night with you?" he asked. "Tomorrow, I go north."

They made him welcome. When they asked who he was, he replied: "I am Sketco, the Raven," but they had never heard of him.

"You will tell your children stories about my doings," Sketco said with a smile. "I am going to teach Atsentma to be more generous."

"The Game Mother will not listen to you," said the hunters skeptically.

"Did you ever hear of the chief who kept all the light to himself, hidden in two boxes and tied up in a bag?" asked the Raven, grinning slyly and watching their puzzled faces. "Did you ever hear of Qok, the great Snowy Owl?"

Their faces were blank, and long after Sketco was asleep, they sat gossiping and speculating about their strange guest, while the fires burned low and the wolves howled under the glittering stars.

In the morning, Sketco took leave of them and before their astonished eyes turned into the shape of a great black bird. With mouths and eyes wide open, they watched him sailing into the North, and when, in the months to follow, the game fell to their hands, they remembered what he had told them.

As he flew above the barrens of the North, the Raven's sharp eyes caught sight of a herd of caribou on the march far below him, on the run, moving as unitedly and intently as an army, so closely massed that the antlers of the animals resembled a forest of dead branches, a forest stripped by fire and wind and bleached by the sun, a forest crawling across the grey plain. To the Raven, the herd appeared to be creeping steadily but slowly, but the caribou were running faster than a hunter could follow.

"Ah!" said Sketco, balancing himself on his broad wings and beginning to circle slowly, "they are rushing to the Game Mother! I will keep my eye on them and they shall lead me to her house."

As he watched, he saw a pack of wolves padding along in the same direction, and he could make out the shaggy forms of bears lurching forward at great speed.

"She is calling them home," Sketco mused. "No wonder the poor mortals are starving. Ah! there go the deer! And those giants ambling along, are they moose? Yes, moose! And elk! The whole world seems to be moving north!"

At last the Raven caught sight of Atsentma's lodge,

solitary in the wilderness, and like a stone, he dropped out of the sky at her door.

It was in the form of a man that he made himself known to the Game Mother. "Who are you?" she asked suspiciously, with black eyes glaring at him from behind the untidy locks of her lank hair.

"I am a great traveller," said Sketco, politely. "All I ask is a little food — a little gossip."

"I have no gossip," said the Game Mother, shutting her jaw with a snap and scowling at him.

"May I have a morsel to eat? I have travelled many miles, and I am famished."

Grudgingly, Atsentma offered him food and squatted near him, watching him closely as he ate.

"You mistrust me," Sketco said quietly, without looking at her.

"I am not used to having visitors," the woman said curtly.

"You should be pleased to see me, then!" Sketco turned and smiled at her ingratiatingly. But her morose face did not lighten.

"What do you want?" she demanded.

The Raven shrugged his shoulders.

"I told you I was a traveller."

"Don't lie. Nobody ever comes here. There is nothing to see."

Sketco raised his eyebrows. "The Northern Lights?" he suggested. "You have a good view here."

Atsentma snorted and Sketco turned away to smile.

Suddenly he turned to her. "I came to see your game, Atsentma."

The woman started. With one hand she brushed back the thick hair from her face, and leaned over to look into his eyes. "Are you a hunter?" she asked grimly. The Raven had scarcely time to utter "No," before she seized him by the neck with her long fingers.

So violent was the attack that Sketco was thrown off his balance and he tumbled over backward with the woman on top of him thrusting her thumbs into his throat. But as quickly as he fell he was on his feet again and with a desperate jerk he sent the Game Mother staggering. She fell in a heap on the ground, and there she grovelled, breathless.

Sketco stood grinning at her. "No, I am not a hunter," he said. "I am a wrestler. Why are you so jealous of your game?" he asked. "Do you think no one has any animals but you?"

"I own all the animals," said Atsentma in a hoarse voice. She looked up at him defiantly.

Sketco laughed. "I know your little herds! Where I come from, the woods and plains are thick with game, and the animals owe no allegiance to you. They have never even heard your name."

The Game Mother sprang to her feet, scowling and clenching her fists. "You lie! I own all the animals!"

Again Sketco laughed. "Keep your temper," said he. "I am not to be frightened by your screams. Or your fingers," he added, rubbing his throat and grinning. "You think you have made us suffer by calling your game home, but we have plenty."

"All the animals are here. They come when I call and do as I say."

"You cannot cheat me," said the Raven. "You only cheat yourself when you think the game obeys you."

"Whoever you are, you are a liar and a fool," said Atsentma grimly. "I will prove to you that all my game has come home."

The Raven lifted an eyebrow dubiously and shrugged his shoulders. But this was just what he desired.

"Come and stand beside me," said the Game Mother, and she went to the door and rounded her mouth for a long hoarse call. Shaking the earth with the thunder of their hooves, the caribou drove past Atsentma's hut, closely crowded together, tails straight up in the air. The herd seemed endless and Sketco was so fatigued with standing that he would have sat down gladly, but the Game Mother stood beside him, tireless.

When the last tail vanished, the Game Mother turned to the Raven with a triumphant leer on her lips. Sketco shrugged his shoulders as if to say: "Perhaps I was wrong about the caribou . . ."

Changing her voice, Atsentma called the deer, and she summoned the moose to parade before her and the Raven; the caribou, the deer, the moose, the bears, the elk, all the game that she controlled filed past her door in thousands upon thousands, until Sketco's ears were ringing with the din, his eyes were swollen with dust and his legs would no longer hold him upright.

"Now where are your boasts and lies?" the Game Mother asked derisively. "These are all my children."

"I was wrong," confessed the weary Raven, humbly. "I honour you, Great Mother. Will you call the chiefs of all these tribes before you, so that I may honour them, too?"

Atsentma called and whistled and the chiefs of all the animals answered obediently and stood in a circle before her door.

"They are all assembled," said the Game Mother with smug satisfaction. "Chiefs!" she called out to the animals. "This great traveller from the South has come to pay you homage."

The chiefs snorted and murmured and pawed the ground. With a hideous smirk, Atsentma turned to the Raven and then addressed the black Bear. "Chief of the Bears," she said, "this great traveller is a famous wrestler. He would do you honour by trying a fall with you."

"Oh, no!" cried Sketco, pretending alarm. "I was only boasting when I said I was a wrestler."

The big black Bear, who had shuffled forward out of the ring and stood swaying on his hind legs, questioned the Game Mother with his little black eyes.

Atsentma laughed. "I thought we'd get the truth when he saw how long your arms were, Chief!" she said. "He is only brave when he tackles old women!"

"I am not afraid of his long arms," Sketco said, "but I do think his legs are too long." The Bear, indeed, seemed as tall as a totem pole. "Nevertheless, I will pay my respects to him by accepting his challenge."

The Game Mother squatted down on her haunches to watch, and the animal chiefs stood still.

When the Raven stepped forward, the Bear lunged at

147

him, arms outstretched. His weight would have crushed Sketco's ribs and snapped his spine, but Sketco nimbly skipped aside and the Bear crashed into a tree. For a moment, he was stunned. Sketco leapt on his back and dug his fingers into the deep fur.

With a mighty shrug, the Bear shook him off and turned to scoop him from the ground with his great paw. But Sketco was not there. He dodged behind Atsentma and called out, "Here I am! Come and catch me!"

Like an avalanche, the near-sighted Bear hurled himself at the only shape he could see, and that was the Game Mother. She yelled and just managed to jump out of the way and save her life. The animal chiefs stirred uneasily as the Bear came plunging into their midst.

He stood up, his wicked little eyes burning with rage, and faced Sketco. "Why don't you grapple with me, mighty Chief?" the Raven taunted. He danced from side to side until the Bear was dizzy, turning his head this way and that to see him.

All of a sudden, Sketco threw himself at the Bear, his head like a battering ram, and knocked the wind out of the animal. While he lay breathless, the Raven grasped his hind legs, one after the other, and snapped the bones. "Your legs are too long," he said. "Bears should not be able to leap over the ground like rabbits. You may keep the strength of your arms, but I am shortening your legs to give the hunters a chance."

Atsentma ground her teeth as the Bear went hobbling away to join the other chiefs. They were now restless and beginning to grow frightened, and she was opening her mouth to order them back into the forest when Sketco said, "I would like to pay my respects to the Caribou People."

The Caribou Chief could not help himself. He was apprehensive, but he stepped forward, looking doubtfully from Atsentma to the Raven.

"Why do you run so fast?"

The Caribou gave him a frightened glance and turned in appeal to the Game Mother.

"Lift up your leg. Ah!" the Raven exclaimed, taking one of the animal's forelegs in his hand and feeling it with his fingers. "You have no fat below the knee. You are too swift, my friend. No wonder the hunters cannot follow you!"

He took a handful of fat from the Caribou's thigh and slapped it on his thin leg. "From this day forward," said the Raven, "you and your tribe will travel a little more slowly."

The Caribou looked reproachfully at the Game Mother as he went back to the circle of chiefs, but she could only glower. She could do nothing against Sketco's magic.

In different ways the Raven hampered the speed of all the animals. The last was the Deer, which did not wait to be called but turned with a spring and bounded off into the forest.

"Stop!" cried Sketco.

The chief of the Deer stopped and turned to look at him, swivelling his long ears to listen.

"You are fleet-footed," said the Raven, "and fleet-footed you shall remain, but you shall not altogether escape your duty to the race of Man. Timid you may be, you Deer People, and nervous and swift-springing, but I will weaken you with curiosity. Hereafter, while you run from the hunter, you must slacken speed from time to time and turn to look at him. Man shall not be as swift as you, but your foolish curiosity will help him."

At last, when all the animals had been changed, Sketco turned to Atsentma and said: "Game Mother, they are yours to command as before, but you must not keep them in the barren North where they can be of no use to anyone. Sometimes, you may call them home to you, but you must let them go again, to wander where mankind can reach them. Now send them southward."

Atsentma held her neck and her jaw rigid and said "No!" with her defiant eyes, but at last she quailed under the Raven's steady gaze and signalled the animals to leave her.

"Now," said the Raven, "you must give me something to eat, for I have a long flight before me."

Greatly humbled, the Game Mother followed him into the house.

CHAPTER 12

THE RAVEN AND THE GRIZZLY BEAR

Far spent after many wanderings, the Raven one day staggered into a village, seeking rest and comfort, only to be met by such wailing and lamentation as he had never heard before.

"What grieves you?" he asked one old woman, who sat with her arms crossed, rocking to and fro and weeping.

The old woman went on swaying and crying and was not able to answer.

"What troubles you?" Sketco asked a younger woman, who was also crouched in misery.

But the young woman could not speak. The Raven asked his question over and over again, with the same result, until a blind old man, hearing his voice, hobbled out and said: "Who comes? I hear a stranger's voice."

"It is Sketco, the Raven. Why is your village in such distress, old man?"

"The men are out hunting and the women sit and

weep," said the old man in a quavering voice. "I am old and blind or I would be out hunting, too!" he exclaimed, his weak voice rising as he clenched his skinny hands. "The Grizzly has taken eight of our young boys. And he carries off our young girls. Night after night, he steals into the village, and he never goes away without killing. When our strong men attack him, he smashes them to the earth with one blow of his arm and breaks every bone in their bodies." The blind man finished in a groan.

"I will help you," said Sketco. "Give me something to eat, for I have come many miles, tramping and flying, and I am worn out."

The old man did not hear him, but two small boys ran and brought him food and drink. He sat down and ate ravenously and then, to the surprise of everyone — the women even stopped weeping in their amazement — rose up and changed his shape and flew off over the village.

Sketco circled slowly, peering to left and to right with his sharp eyes, and at last he caught sight of the hunting party creeping down the hill.

He dropped into the midst of the men, who were dragging themselves heavily and dejectedly homeward, and if they had not been so weary they would have killed him, he startled them so.

"Have no fear!" he said cheerfully in his man's tongue, as he looked into their frightened eyes. "I am Sketco, the Raven. I found your village sunk in desolation and I am ready to help you. You have not killed the Grizzly?"

He need not have asked the question, for the answer could be read plainly in their drooping shoulders.

"We have not killed the Grizzly," said one of the hunters. "We took our Shaman with us to destroy him with his medicine but he has clawed the Shaman into tatters. What can we do if the magic of the medicine men is not strong enough to daunt him?"

"There is stronger medicine than the shaking of a rattle," replied the Raven.

"Our Chief lies dead in his den," bewailed another man, "and the bones of our young sons and daughters are scattered as thick as dead branches in the river when winter is going out."

"There is a new Chief," a gaunt man said brusquely.

"He ran away!" someone spat with disgust.

"Had he not kept himself apart, you would have no leader at all!" The gaunt man turned on him sharply and scowled into his face. "There is nobody else fit to lead. Follow! And with mouths shut."

"Soon you will have no followers," said the rebellious man. "Safe in your skin, you can lead the women in weeping."

The new Chief would have struck him, but Sketco put up his hand.

"The real chief of this tribe," he said, "appears to be the Grizzly. I will kill him for you."

The rebellious man measured him with his eyes. "If you can kill the Grizzly," he said calmly, "we will make you Chief."

The gaunt man looked at him darkly and then turned a sinister eye on Sketco.

"Must I fight the two of them?" the Raven asked himself. The men went down as he clambered up the hill, following a trail of blood.

The trail of blood became a trail of bones and at length Sketco stood peering into a dark cavern which was half hidden by two huge boulders and which stank evilly.

"Are you at home, Grizzly Man?" he asked softly. He could hear the monster breathing heavily and snuffling and cracking bones in his teeth. Sketco's heart beat in his throat.

He heard the Grizzly snort. The monster stopped eating and sniffed loudly. Sketco dodged behind one of the rocks and squeezed down, trembling. He was afraid that the bear might hear his heart thumping.

The Grizzly waddled out of his lair, an enormous shaggy beast whose fur was tipped with silver, and he had blood on his muzzle and on his long claws.

"One stroke from that arm, and I should be crushed like the paper nest of a wasp," thought Sketco, crouching lower and staring at the bear with wide-open eyes. The Grizzly sniffed to right and left and reared up to a tremendous height on his hind legs, swaying and pawing the air and sniffing greedily, and blinking his wicked little eyes. Sketco shuddered. At last the bear slumped down and ambled into his den, and soon the Raven heard him crunching bones again and sucking and snuffling.

Sketco straightened out his stiff legs and wiped the sweat off his forehead. He settled down more comfortably and for a long time he sat behind the boulder, straining his ears, and straining his wits to think of a way to destroy the fierce creature that was now sleeping sluggishly after his meal and breathing so heavily a few feet away.

"No magic I know would as much as scratch him," thought Sketco. "I must trick him."

Gathering up all his courage, he went to the mouth of the den again and whispered: "Are you at home, Grizzly Man?"

There was no answer, but the Grizzly stopped snoring. He came out of the cavern so swiftly and so quietly that Sketco fell back aghast.

He was horrified to see that it was not a bear that stood before him, blinking sleepily, but a man. And the man was Sketco's uncle.

"Oh!" the Raven gasped and then pressed his fingers against his lips in fright for having cried out.

The Grizzly Man blinked his wicked little eyes as if the light bothered him. When he saw Sketco, he smiled with his strong yellow teeth and said: "Yes, I am at home. Come into my house. You are welcome."

He did not know that the young man who stood before him was the nephew he had tried to drown in the sea in the same way as he had drowned the three brothers.

The Raven's mind worked quickly.

"No, I will not come in," he said. "I am in a hurry. I came to warn you, Grizzly Man."

The uncle studied Sketco's face and said nothing. "A young man is coming to kill you."

"Ho! ho! ho!" The Grizzly Man suddenly burst out laughing. "Ho! ho! ho! Ho! ho! ho!" He held his sides and looked down at Sketco out of eyes filled with the tears of laughter. "Do you know what I do with young men who come to kill me?" He pulled up a young spruce by the roots and snapped it in two with his fingers. Then he bit into one of the pieces of wood and spat out a mouthful of splinters.

Sketco trembled but said: "This man comes from the North in a flying canoe."

The Grizzly Man stopped pulling a splinter out of his teeth and looked at Sketco.

"He says: 'Three were drowned but the fourth saved himself.'"

The Grizzly Man suddenly clutched Sketco by the shoulder. The Raven winced. He felt as if his bones were being broken.

"Where is this brave young man?"

"He has many shapes," said the Raven, screwing up his face with pain. "Let me go, Grizzly Man, and I will tell you."

Sketco's uncle released him and stood breathing heavily and leaning down over him threateningly. "I have grown lusty up here in the hills," he growled. "I am not afraid of his magic. Tell me where he is and I will crush him until he spits his heart out!"

"He has m-many shapes," the Raven stuttered. His mouth was so dry that he could hardly speak. "N-n-now he is a fire!"

"A fire?"

"A mighty, roaring fire!"

The Grizzly Man lurched forward, "Where? I will scatter him into the river!" He threw his arm out so violently that if Sketco had not dodged he would have been struck down.

"You could not find him," said Sketco, "he sleeps in a small stone, so small that you could never discover him, unless you were told where to look. But tonight, at the village, he will leap out and dance madly, flaring and boasting, shouting to the sky. Come then and plunge into the midst of the fire and you can rake his heart out of the flames and so destroy your cunning enemy."

"Huh," said the Grizzly Man gruffly. "I will put an end to him." He grinned suddenly. "Why did you come to tell me this? To save yourself from my claws and my teeth, eh, little man?" He snatched at Sketco, but Sketco was too quick for him. "You will taste all the sweeter for being such a tender young fellow!" growled the Grizzly with grim humour.

With a quick lunge forward, the monster grabbed at Sketco, but he wriggled out of his reach. The Grizzly Man's nails scratched his thigh and drew blood, but the Raven smiled.

"Tonight!" he called as he ran down the hill. "You will see the fire dancing madly and hear him shouting to the sky. Throw yourself upon him and tear out his heart!"

When he reached the village, the Raven ran into the gaunt Chief's house. "I have a scheme!" he cried. "I have tricked the Grizzly Man!"

The men of the tribe crowded in to hear him and the wails of the women were hushed.

"When the Grizzly Man comes tonight, you are to be ready for him with a big . . ."

"Who are you, to come to us with your tricks?" the Chief asked coldly.

"If you do not wish to be saved from the monster," Sketco said angrily, "I will kill him for reasons of my own."

"We can kill the Grizzly without your tricks," said the Chief.

"You had better kill him soon, then, before he devours the rest of the village! Why have you not saved your Chief from him, and your Shaman?"

"We have a new Chief and a new Medicine Man."

The rebellious man rose. "If the stranger kills the Grizzly," he announced in a loud voice, "he will be the new Chief. We need men who stay and fight, not men who run away, to be our leaders."

There was a murmur of approval as he turned on his heel and walked out.

The new Chief glared at Sketco malevolently. "This man is a devil," he said to his followers. "He comes, as a black bird, from nowhere. What brings him here?"

"He is in league with the Grizzly," said a young man who now pushed his way to the front. His hair was long and he wore a bone through his nose. In his hand he carried a rattle. "He is in league with the Grizzly," said the new Shaman. "He has come to destroy us while pretending to save us."

"That is a lie!" said Sketco hotly.

The men muttered.

The new Chief spoke solemnly. "Do you believe the words of your Shaman and of your Chief, or are you deceived by the tongue of this boastful stranger? I am accused of cowardice because I withdrew and saved myself from the Grizzly to lead you. What good is a dead Chief? You have many already. Do they help you in time of trouble? I knew I was to be Chief, so I saved myself for you."

The hunters and the women agreed.

"I have new plans for killing the Grizzly, since the old plans failed. And since the old magic failed, the new Shaman has new magic."

Sketco swallowed his anger.

"We must first of all kill this stranger before he betrays us," insinuated the Medicine Man.

The hunters shouted "Kill him!" and sprung up. The Shaman reached out to seize Sketco's arm, but the arm became a wing and the Raven flashed out of the house through the doorway, taking to flight as a shower of arrows was hurtled at him.

With a sore heart, he flew away from the village.

That night, the Grizzly stole down again lifting his head and sniffing, rearing up on his hind legs and sniffing. But he smelt no smoke. He heard no crackling of flames and he saw no fire.

"Where is that slippery young man who came to warn me? He will make a tasty morsel."

But he could not find the Raven, and in his rage he tore through the village, playing havoc with every household. No one ever knew what the new Chief's plans might have been, or the new Shaman's magic.

CHAPTER 13

THE RAVEN PAINTS THE BIRDS FOR WAR

Far away from the ravaged village, Sketco sat on a stone with his chin on his hands and brooded. "Do such people deserve to be saved?" he asked himself gloomily. "I come to risk my life and save them, and how do they reward me? If I had not been so swift, they would have murdered me."

He sat looking out over the lake. A beaver was swimming silently under the water close to shore, but he did not see him; nor did he see the family of ducks that was out for an evening swim.

"Is it the fault of the people? Or does the blame rest upon the leaders? Pah!" he exclaimed contemptuously. "The people are like a drift of leaves before the wind. The wind blows north, and north they go; south the wind blows, and they go south; and when the wind dies down, they lie where they have fallen."

He rose so suddenly that the beaver, who had put his head above the water to look at him, dived down as if he had been shot, slapping the water with such a resounding noise as he dived that the ducks fled in terror and Sketco was jerked out of his dream.

"The innocent," he said, "suffer with the guilty, and because of the innocent I will kill the Grizzly. If I had never found this stricken village, I must kill the Grizzly for the sake of my murdered brothers."

He walked along the shore, skimming pebbles across the lake and trying to think of a plan. He had not gone far before he stopped, struck by an idea. He whistled shrilly.

The ducks pricked up their heads and looked at him. He whistled again and the ducks swam toward him. A different note he whistled, and the two nighthawks that were zigzagging across the sky with rasping cries dipped down and hovered over his head.

"Ducks and Nighthawks," said Sketco. "Await me here. I am calling all the birds to war. I am Sketco, the Raven, and I have declared war on the Grizzly. I need your help."

He whistled shrilly and softly, sweetly and piercingly, long notes and short notes, with his fingers and through his teeth, and from all quarters of the heavens the birds came to him. The Loons came hooting and scooting across the lake; a flight of Geese sailed out of the night in a graceful line; the Ospreys and the Eagles dropped down out of the sky; the great Snowy Owl settled on the beach like a snowdrift from the ultimate North; the Robins came, strutting pompously; and chattering Sparrows and Starlings; the Bluebirds from the mountains and the Larks from the prairies and the Gulls from the sea; the forests poured out the Siskins and the Phoebes and the Whitethroats, the Jays and the Woodpeckers; the Kingfisher came from the river and the ragged, flapping Crows lounged across the sky, cawing rudely, and the Blackbirds came and the Grackles and the swerving Swallows. No bird was missing, not the Finch, nor the Hummingbird, nor the Grosbeak, nor the Waxwing, nor the Thrasher, nor the Catbird, nor the Sandpiper, nor the Quail, nor the Pigeon, nor the Prairie Chicken, nor the Heron, nor the Redpoll, nor the Warbler, nor the Kinglet, nor the Shrike; Cuckoo and Whippoorwill, Bobolink and Whooping Crane, Gannet and Tern.

In those days, they were all different from each other, as they are today, except for their colours. The Robin was portly and full of pomposity; the Sparrows were small and saucy; the Eagle was big and ruthless, with a piercing eye and a beak like a steel trap; the Finches were dainty and frivolous; the Geese were lordly but good-natured; the Crows were disreputable vagabonds, and the Thrashers and the Waxwings and the Swallows were sleek and beautifully mannered; the Gulls were complaining and quarrelsome; the Loon was flamboyant and melancholy; the Pigeons were stupid and the Catbird was cunning; some stalked on stilts, some waddled on scarcely any legs at all; some had blunt bills and some had beaks sharper than spearheads; some nested on the crags and explored the clouds and some dwelt timidly in the rushes or in the deep grass; some laughed like mad things, some shrieked, some whistled and trilled and sang lovely songs, some squawked and some only peeped. They all had their ways which made them different from each other, but they were all of the same colours: some white, some black and some brown.

The air was full of wings, white and black and brown, beating against the sky with a noise like thunder (but the Thunder Man had not been asked) and the lake echoed with whistles and wails and shrieks and rasping, throaty cries: the *mahonk* of Geese, and the *quawquawk* of Ducks, the *Canadacanadacanada* of the Whitethroat, the *tirril-tirril-tirrillee-tirril* of the Robins, the *Polly-polly-put-on-your-teaket-*

tle-ettle! of the Meadowlarks; with *phoebees* and *caws* and *coos* and *hoos* and such a chattering and a jabbering that Sketco had to put his hands over his ears to shut out the noise while he lifted his own voice as loudly as he could and shouted for silence.

It was no use; they could not hear him. So he went down to the water's edge, knelt on the sand and summoned the Beaver.

"Old Man Beaver," he said, "come up and help me. I have called these birds together so that I may give them orders for the war against the Grizzly and now I cannot make them hear."

Old Man Beaver shook the water out of his whiskers, blinked, and dived under the water to his house beneath the heap of branches the Beaver People had gnawed down with their strong teeth. When he appeared again, he was followed by his household and by all the Beaver People in the lake. Together they swam out to the middle. Suddenly, they all dived at once. The slap of a hundred flat tails made such a mighty explosion that all the birds fell as quiet as if a cold wind had passed through the woods and up the sky, freezing them stiff where they hung. Fear had struck them dumb.

"Thank you, Beaver," said the Raven, lifting his hand.

He turned to the birds.

"My friends," he said gravely, "we are gathered here to make war."

At once there was a great tumult. Some of the birds screamed for joy, some of them croaked grimly, some of them complained and cried that they had better things to do. Sketco held up his hand to hush the hubbub.

"The enemy is as venomous as he is fierce," said the Raven. "I must rid the world of him, and you must all help me. I will paint you for battle and we will sweep down upon him and strike terror into his heart. We will sweep down out of the sky like a cloud of wings and beaks and claws and tear him to pieces, until not a shred of his vile body is left and he can do no more harm."

The excitement of the birds knew no bounds. They were all curious to know what colours they were to be painted. They were jealous of one another and some of them pushed forward greedily and yelled "Me first! Paint me yellow! Paint me red! Paint me with stripes!" But Sketco heeded none of them, except to push them back, and went on with his work.

All night the Raven painted, under the light of the moon and, when the moon went, in the early dawn. His paints were squeezed out of the roots of trees and weeds and out of flower blossoms and out of the earth itself.

He stained the Robin's breast with the juice of berries and the Robin puffed out his ample chest with greater pomposity than ever and strutted among the birds as if he were chief of them all. "Perhaps I will make him Chief," thought Sketco, a little deceived at first by his showiness, but when he saw the airs the Robin put on, he changed his mind.

To punish the Robin for his vanity, the Raven called out the smallest bird of all, the Hummingbird, and painted him into a living jewel.

"Who is this mite who is being painted so gorgeously?" jeered the Robin.

"All I see is a blur of wings," the Eagle said.

"Is it a wasp?" asked the Flycatcher.

It was delicate work, painting the tiny creature, not only because it was so small but because it moved so quickly and would not be still.

"He shall live among the flowers," said Sketco proudly, "himself a flower without roots." He was so engrossed in his painting that he seemed to have forgotten the Grizzly. "He shall suck nectar from them."

"A sort of bee!" the Robin sneered. "I thought we were being painted for war! What harm can this insect do? Live among the flowers! Himself a flower! An insipid vegetarian, that is what he is! Sucking nectar. *I eat meat!* And you can depend upon me in a fight."

He shrugged his wings contemptuously and sauntered off to patronize the Blackbirds, but the Blackbirds only laughed at him and he turned away, very much offended.

Sketco painted the Loon splendidly in black and white and hung a string of shells about his neck. "Now, my fine fellow," he said, "with your voice and your swiftness, you will make a mighty fighter." But the Loon turned and fled, laughing eerily, across the lake.

Sketco was surprised and disappointed, but he kept on with his work, lavishing his most gorgeous colours on the crested Wood Duck; dipping the Mallard's head in green dye and the solemn-nosed Canvas-Back's in rusty red; tinging the Grackle's black neck with a splendid shimmering purple; combing up the Merganser's handsome white hood and edging it delicately with black. He became so happy painting that he forgot all about the stricken village and the Grizzly and his desperate purpose. He laughed as he picked up the stocky Puffin and dipped its preposterous bill into bright red paint, whitened its face and stretched out its yellowish tuft. All the other birds who were not busy admiring themselves or trying to steal Sketco's colours to bedeck themselves, laughed, too, and the poor Puffin, overcome with shame, took to his wings and went off to the sea.

But Sketco was freakishly streaking the Harlequin Duck with white, and he did not see the discomfiture of the ridiculous Puffin.

"Paint us! Paint us!" chattered the Sparrows. But they made such a nuisance of themselves that he left them a nondescript rusty brown and black, while he brushed the Finches lightly with a sprig of Goldenrod and dipped the Bluebird into a little puddle that had been holding secret for days the reflection of the sunny sky. As one of the Blackbirds flew in his face to tease him, he dabbed a spot of scarlet on its wings, but the Crows perched on dead branches high above his head, mockingly caw-cawing and refusing to be painted. To one of the Eagles he gave a white crown; he drew the Jay's hair up into a topknot; spattered some of the Woodpeckers gloriously with black and white and gave some of them crimson heads; speck-led the Flicker's breast and gave him a moustache and a handsome gorget.

As Sketco painted, the birds made a great clamour, showing off their new feathers to make their neighbours envious, laughing or jeering at each other, or trying to thrust themselves into Sketco's fingers, impatient for their turn. Perhaps if it had not been for the aggressive King-bird, who chased them away, the Crows would have con-descended to be painted with the others, but as it was, they pretended to be above such folly. The black and white Kingbird, however, gained nothing by his pugnacity except a small patch of orange on his pate that no one could see unless he was greatly excited.

The Raven went on with his work, quickly and happily, almost haphazardly. He murmured with delight when he had dyed the Orioles orange and the Martins purple, when he ringed the Killdeer with a beautiful dou-ble collar, or when he watched the rich black run down the long neck of the Canada Goose. He laughed when he put goggles on the Peregrine Falcon and when he wrapped a striped fur round the Barred Owl and gave the fat, se-date Grouse its ruff. He worked in yellows when he came to the Warblers, speckled the Larks and the Sandpipers; some birds he tinted delicately, some he mottled, some he striped boldly.

The work went on and the birds were restless and noisy and quarrelsome. When the sun rose, the Owls disappeared so silently that no one saw them slip away.

"I'm sick of this!" the Robin suddenly announced,

peevish because Sketco was not paying any attention to him. "Am I not Chief here?"

The birds cackled and laughed and screamed at him, and his red chest blushed ruddier than ever. "Why should I stay only to be insulted?"

"You are not Chief here," said Sketco quietly, without looking up. He was carefully brushing the Junco's grey wings.

"I need not trouble you any more, then," said the Robin testily.

The other birds hooted at him, so he flew up to a branch on a tall tree and sat gazing down scornfully. When no one was looking, he vanished.

"Am I Chief?" the Eagle asked truculently.

"There is no Chief," said Sketco, looking up and suddenly remembering his war. He jumped to his feet. "I will lead. Bird People!" he called. "No more painting. It is time to fight. Prepare yourselves!"

"I follow no lead," said the Eagle proudly, and with that he dived into the air and soared toward the sun.

The birds then all began to fight among themselves, each claiming to be leader, and they began attacking Sketco and demanding food.

"We are hungry!" they shouted. "Give us something

to eat! How much longer must we stay here? When does the battle begin? Give us something to eat! Give us flies! Give us worms! Give us seeds! Give us fish! Give us mice! Give us caterpillars, beetles, grasshoppers!"

"You shall have a great feast when the Grizzly is killed," the Raven promised. "I have worked hard all night. I have painted you splendidly. Will you fail me now?"

"Are we splendid?" asked the Sparrows. "Ragamuffins! That's all we are! Why did you not make us golden like the Finches? or give us pretty skull-caps like you gave the Red-polls and the Kinglets?"

They swarmed round Sketco, jabbering and darting at him, until he had to fend them off with his hands. The Crows flapped away, jeering at the whole business, while the G____ ___ the sea so petulantly that the Raven said to _____ must! You never were much help to me!" The ____ ____ped into the lake and began nosing into the weeds, and the Geese, after a consultation among themselves, presented their respects and told Sketco that they were afraid they must be going as winter was coming and they had to face a long flight to the South. This made the other birds more restless and the whole lakeside was in an uproar.

At last Sketco brandished a stick at the birds that

were left. "Begone!" he cried. "You are a pack of useless, ungrateful animals! Go, or I will break your wings and you will never fly again!"

There was a great scurry and piping and peeping and a terrific rush of wings as all the birds, great and small, took to flight. Some soared high above the trees, others disappeared into the woods, and some dived into the water.

"Go and get your food!" said Sketco bitterly. "Eating is all you think about."

He turned his back on the lake, jumped into the air and flew off toward the Grizzly's den on the hillside.

CHAPTER 14

HOW SKETCO TRICKED THE GRIZZLY

Sketco avoided the village, flew over it and dropped to earth at the mouth of the Grizzly Man's cave. The monster was sleeping within, but he awakened with a start when Sketco, in human shape once more, flung a stone at him.

The uncle rushed out of his den. His thick hair was tousled and he blinked in the sun as if his eyes had not yet become used to the light.

"Who is this, waking me up so early in the morning?" he grumbled. "He had better be careful, for I have been dreaming evil dreams, and I am in an ugly mood!"

"It is Sketco," answered the Raven, "the boy you drowned."

The Bear Man rubbed his eyes and at last saw the Raven standing in front of him with folded arms. The youth was sturdily planted on both feet and the sun made his dusky skin glow.

"Drowned?" growled the Grizzly.

"No!" Sketco laughed. "You thought you had drowned me, but do you remember your surprise when you came into my mother's house after the fishing trip, and I was there to greet you?"

The uncle scowled and took a step forward.

"You are the same young man who came to warn me . . ."

"Against myself! To warn you that I was tracking you down!" Sketco put back his head and laughed merrily. "I told you I was playing the part of Fire."

"I saw no fires," said the Grizzly. He had eaten too much and slept badly and his wits were muddled. "Are you my nephew?"

"I am your nephew," Sketco replied.

"You came here to murder me," said the Grizzly Man hoarsely.

"Are you surprised at that? You fled from my mother's house. I have searched the world for you. My brothers are dead."

"Many others are dead, too! And dying every day!" He lurched forward and seized Sketco's shoulders with two strong arms. He bared his teeth and glared into Sketco's eyes.

177

But the Raven held his ground and did not flinch.

"I am not safe until you are one of them. You shall not escape so easily, my clever fellow!"

"Do not forget my magic," said the Raven quietly. "Look behind you."

The Grizzly released Sketco and wheeled round in a panic.

"You cannot see it," said Sketco. "Your eyes are too small."

Grizzly Man cowered, trembling, and stared at the Raven with scared eyes.

"Do not be frightened," said Sketco with a smile. "It will not lay hands on you if you do not touch me. But the moment you raise a finger against me it will pounce on you and it will grind you to dust, even to your very soul."

Grizzly Man glanced around uneasily and then he smiled with a sickly leer and said: "Raven, you and I are too clever and too strong to be enemies. Let us be friends."

"You say that when you know I have the advantage. If I showed a weak spot and gave you the chance, you would forget those words. If I turned my back, you would betray me."

"Come into my house," said the bear amiably, "and let

us have a feast together."

"I will not go into your filthy den."

The Grizzly looked at him with hatred.

"And I do not eat the flesh of men."

The Grizzly smiled, but his smile was worse than his black look of enmity. He shrugged his shoulders and sat down on the ground. "Very well, I must entertain you here, in the sunlight."

"That's better," Sketco said. "But I am hungry. Let us go and get some salmon. I have a harpoon that never misses. The head is made out of a ghost's rib."

The Grizzly Man watched the Raven's movements as he picked up the spear which he had stuck in the ground and poised it in his hand as if to strike.

"Come," said Sketco. Grizzly Man rose and together they went down the hill on the other side, tramping all day and eating berries along the way.

"Your river is far," said the Grizzly suspiciously, time and time again, and Sketco always answered: "The best fish are always far to seek."

By nightfall, they heard the roar of the water and at last came to the brink of the canyon through which the river raved. After Sketco had plunged his harpoon into the water several times and brought out three or four gasping, lashing salmon, they went up to an open space above the river and made a fire to cook the catch.

At every move, Sketco watched the Grizzly and the Grizzly watched Sketco, each fearful of the other. But the Raven was careful to show no sign of weakness, nervous as he was. Once he turned in time to catch his uncle standing over him with a big stone in his hand ready to crush his skull in. When Sketco looked into his eyes, the bear smiled feebly and let the stone drop. Sketco said nothing, but he did not sleep that night.

The Grizzly tried to remain awake, too, fearful of being murdered in his sleep, but weariness overcame him.

When he awoke in the morning and found that he was still alive, he began to think that Sketco meant him no harm after all. But the Raven had a scheme in his mind.

"Heap up the fire," he said. "Make it blazing hot. I have some cooking to do."

While the bear piled branches on the flames, Sketco went about gathering stones. He came back with six, each as large as an apple, and dropped them into the fire.

"What are you doing with the stones?" the Grizzly Man asked curiously.

"Can't you see?" was the reply. "I am baking them."

"Baking stones! Why? I never heard of anyone baking stones!"

"You live too much to yourself, up there in your den on the hill," said Sketco, laying another branch across the fire. "You should go about the world as I do, and learn what is going on."

"I go about too much for some people!" The Grizzly laughed coarsely.

"Have you ever visited the land of the dead?" asked Sketco, sitting down by the fire and poking at it with a stick.

"No," said the Grizzly. He looked behind him apprehensively.

"He is still there," said the Raven, without looking up. "Some day you will," he added.

"Are we not going to eat?" asked the Grizzly nervously.

"Oh, yes, in a little while."

"What is there to eat? The fish is all gone."

"Yes, you ate most of it. You have a big appetite."

"Let's go and catch some more. I am still hungry."

"Did you ever eat stones?"

The Grizzly looked at Sketco stupidly. "Do you mean to tell me you are going to eat those hot stones?"

"There is nothing I like better than baked stones," said

the Raven. He stirred the fire and with his stick jerked out one of the stones. It was so hot that he could not pick it up in his fingers.

"But one of those would burn a hole through your belly!"

Sketco shrugged. "Did you ever try one?"

The astonished bear shook his head.

"Then how do you know?"

He picked up the stone in two sticks, lifted it to his mouth and pretended to swallow it. What he really did was toss it on the ground behind him, but he was so skilful and the bear so near-sighted that he was utterly deceived. He was dumbfounded. He could do nothing but sit blinking and gaping.

Sketco smacked his lips and licked the corners of his mouth with his tongue. "Ah!" he sighed. "That is sweet! Will you have one?"

He fished out another hot stone and pushed it toward his uncle. But the Grizzly Man wet his finger and touched the stone with the tip of it. He drew back, wincing with pain.

"Did you think it would be cool?" asked the Raven. "It is too hot for the fingers, of course, but the stomach is warm to receive it."

He lifted the second stone to his lips and again pretended to gulp it down.

"Sweet! sweet!" he exclaimed. "You must have courage if you are to enjoy the sweet things of this world. They never go to the timorous. I am surprised to see the terrible Grizzly Man is so easily frightened, he who crunches the bones of mighty chiefs and whole villages! Oh, well, if you are afraid to taste the stones, my friend, I shall have to eat them all myself."

The Grizzly Man gulped and blinked.

"And that," Sketco added, sucking his teeth, "will be no hardship."

"Are they good for you?" asked the Grizzly Man.

"They give you strength." The Raven clenched his fist and crooked his elbow. "Do you see that muscle? Is that bad, for a young man?"

"I am getting old," mumbled the bear.

"Then you should eat baked stoned for breakfast. They will keep you young and lusty. *I* shall never grow old."

"I am feeling rather hungry," the bear admitted reluctantly.

"It is foolish to be hungry when there are plenty of baked stones for the eating. They will only be going bad," said Sketco. "I can never eat more than three at one meal."

He raked another out of the fire.

"This one is a bit scorched, but that adds to the flavour."

"Is it . . . a small one?"

"They are all about the same size. When they are too small, they are unripe, you know, and not good for the digestion. This is a beauty! I think I'll finish my meal with it. I need not eat for a week now."

"A week?" asked the Grizzly uncertainly. "But I like eating . . ."

"Well, this will not destroy the appetite of a powerful man like you. I do not need so much nourishment. It will make you able to eat bigger and bigger feasts. It whets the appetite when appetites are as big as yours."

"I . . . perhaps . . . I think I might try one . . . a small one . . . not too hot."

"I wouldn't persuade you against your will," said the cunning Raven, pretending to swallow the third stone and speaking with his tongue in his cheek as if his mouth were full.

"Please give me one," said the Grizzly, who now had a great deal of respect for the Raven and was much milder in his manners.

"The third was the best of all," said Sketco. "The

longer they cook, the better they taste."

"Get me one out!" demanded the bear, a little more gruffly.

"As you will." He pulled another stone out of the fire and lifted it on the two sticks. "Shut your eyes and open your mouth."

The Grizzly Man opened his mouth wide and shut his eyes. He flinched as he felt the heat of the stone on his face, but he kept his head back and his jaws open.

"Wider," said the Raven.

The bear stretched his mouth open still wider.

Sketco dropped the hot stone in.

The Grizzly Man gulped and screamed as it tumbled down his gullet into his stomach. His eyes watered, and he danced up and down with the frightful pain, holding his belly with both hands. Louder and louder he yelled, squirming and jumping, and, throwing himself on the ground, he writhed and rolled in agony.

"This is your punishment," said Sketco coldly, looking down at him. "You will never again murder people and devour them. You will never again drown innocent boys in the sea."

The Grizzly sprang at him, growling and foaming at the mouth, but Sketco stepped back and the bear fell headlong into the fire, which was now burning low. He pulled himself out and began running to the river, but before he had taken three steps he pitched over and fell dead on the ground.

"That is the end of you and all your evil," said the Raven, looking down at his body.

Sketco stood looking at the Grizzly and, thinking of the little boys murdered so long ago, and of the village, laid waste by the monster's greed and wickedness. He thought of Nass-shig-ee-yalth, who tried to keep the sun, the moon and the stars to himself, and of Qok, the Snowy Owl, who hoarded the fire, of Atsentma, the Game Mother, and of the Man Who Sat on the Tide. Then he changed into his Raven shape and soared above the treetops. As he sailed over the village, he could see that it was beginning to stir. Freed of the Grizzly's tyranny, the people who were left were beginning to make a new life for themselves. Sketco remembered that they had asked him to be their Chief, just as the Shark People had wanted him to stay with them and lead them; but he rose higher on his broad black wings and vanished into the North, content to be remembered in their tales.